A TYCO

SECRET

THE SIN CITY TYCOONS SERIES

A TYCOON'S SECRET

THE SIN CITY TYCOONS SERIES

AVERY LAVAL

A Tycoon's Secret is a work of fiction. Names, characters, places, and incidents either are the product of the author's imagination or are used fictitiously. Any resemblance to actual persons, events, or locales is coincidental.

Copyright © 2018 by Avery Laval Books
All rights reserved.
No part of this book may be reproduced in any form or by any electronic or mechanical means, including information storage and retrieval systems, without written permission from the author, except for the use of brief quotations in a book review.

Publisher's Cataloging-in-Publication Data
A Tycoon's Secret : The Sin City Tycoons Series / Avery Laval.
p.____ cm.____
ISBN 978-1-947834-26-2 (Pbk) | 978-1-947834-27-9 (Ebook)
1. Nevada—Fiction. 2. Romance—Fiction. 3. Love—Fiction. I. Title
813'.6—dc23 | LOC PCN 2018935316

Blue Crow Books

Published by Blue Crow Books
an imprint of Blue Crow Publishing, LLC
Chapel Hill, NC
www.bluecrowpublishing.com
Cover Design by Lauren Faulkenberry
Cover Image Credit: InnervisionArt via shutterstock

PRAISE FOR AVERY LAVAL'S SIN CITY TYCOONS SERIES

"What a sparkling gem of a story! I loved it—and can't wait for the rest of this dazzling series!"

—USA TODAY BESTSELLING AUTHOR CAITLIN CREWS

"Avery Laval's first book in her Sin City Tycoons series is a delicious take on the billionaire boss and secretary trope. I was hooked from the first page and loved every emotional, decadent moment. The characters are strong and layered, and I enjoyed how Jenna clashed with Grant. Who doesn't love a good power play between the sexes? When they finally came together, it made me sigh with happiness. This was the perfect, sexy read to take me away for a few hours, and I can't wait to see what's next!"

—NEW YORK TIMES AND USA TODAY BESTSELLING AUTHOR JESSICA CLARE

"An Avery Laval romance is like a ripe cherry drenched in chocolate—delicious, sexy, and utterly addictive!"

NINA LANE, NEW YORK TIMES AND USA TODAY BESTSELLING AUTHOR OF THE SPIRAL OF BLISS SERIES

"Avery Laval has a flair for writing multi-faceted characters who are refreshingly smart and irresistible. A Tycoon's Jewel has just the right amount of smoldering chemistry, Vegas glamour, and delightfully fast-paced plot. A story to be devoured."

TINA ANN FORKNER, AWARD-WINNING AUTHOR
WAKING UP JOY AND THE REAL THING

ALSO BY AVERY LAVAL

THE SIN CITY TYCOONS SERIES

A Tycoon's Jewel

A Tycoon's Rush

A Tycoon's Secret

ACKNOWLEDGMENTS

I believe that men of all religions and women of all creeds deserve love, regardless of their homelands. I further believe that those who can look deep into themselves and find a way to give their hearts freely again after baby loss of any kind deserve love. I'm grateful to the people in my small town who shared firsthand knowledge of both experiences to help me tell Marissa and Khalid's story. This book is dedicated to them.

Writing a story set in the Mideast may not be palatable for all readers. I hope you'll give it a try, but if it's not for you, there are plenty of other wonderful small press romances out there for you to enjoy. Find me at AveryLaval.com and I'll be happy to recommend a wagonload!

Finally, I'd like to give my special thanks to Katie Rose Guest Pryal, my insightful editor. Khalid was the man of my dreams. But with Katie's help, he became a man worthy of Marissa.

PROLOGUE

SOAP AND HAND LOTION. SHAMPOO AND HAIR DYE. GREETING CARDS. Marissa Madden walked through the aisles of her local drugstore hoping against hope none of her brothers would happen by. It was a ridiculous thought, she reminded herself. Las Vegas was a city of two million people, and besides, she was twenty-five years old. Certainly old enough to walk into a pharmacy and buy a pregnancy test without having to explain herself.

Right?

Wrong, she knew at once. Her three brothers had some kind of special sense that always brought them rushing to the scene when she was trying to keep something a secret. And there was no bigger secret than the one she might be dealing with today. For today, she would finally find out if the reason her period was three weeks late was because she and Khalid, the man she'd fallen in love with the moment she'd laid eyes on him a year ago, were expecting a child.

Her heart squeezed a little tighter at the thought. Yes, she knew it would have been better for them both if they'd done everything in the proper order—first the wedding, *then* the pregnancy. But even so, the thought of carrying Khalid's child nearly brought her tears of joy. There was no doubt in her mind that he was the one she was meant to be with forever, and he'd made no secret of the fact that he felt the same way about her. Nor had he hidden his desire to have a large family when the time came. She couldn't wait to get home and share her suspicions with him, to show him the pregnancy test, so that he would be by her side when they got the results. So that they would find out if they were going to be parents together at the exact same moment.

Overwhelmed by the thought, Marissa pulled down test after test, reading the labels on each box, trying to figure out which gave the fastest—and most accurate—reading. To her excited eyes, the words on each package were just garbles of marketing nonsense and pictures of pink and blue lines that meant nothing. In the end, she picked out the one that promised to give an answer in words—"Yes" or "No"—so that she would be sure to understand the results. She paid the cashier without even noticing how much it cost and hurried through the rare desert rainstorm to her car.

As she drove home, windshield wipers frantically batting back and forth, she tried hard to collect her thoughts and forced herself to consider all the possible outcomes ahead. If she weren't pregnant, then she and Khalid would just go on the way they had been, spending every second not consumed by his pursuit of a business degree and her budding marketing career with each other. She would keep getting to know him even better and daydreaming about the day he would come to her with a ring and ask her to be his wife.

But if she were carrying his child? Would he drop to one knee there in her little black-and-white-tiled bathroom and propose marriage on the spot? Or was there a chance he'd be displeased, and balk at his responsibilities? Marissa forced herself to consider this possibility—she had to be realistic, no matter how hard it was to imagine. But that response seemed so uncharacteristic of Khalid, who believed more than anything in the importance of family. Still, she reminded herself, this pregnancy, if she were indeed pregnant, was unplanned. She had to give thought to the possibility that it would not be well received. After all, they were both right in the middle of pursuing their professional goals, and they had only been together for a year—though it felt as if she'd known him forever. And they'd been taking precautions when they made love in order to avoid this very thing.

But surely Khalid would understand that sometimes, life found a way to break through even the most stalwart precautions. And when two people were meant to be together, it didn't matter if everything happened exactly as it was supposed to. All that mattered was that they took what came at them as a team, side by side.

With a start Marissa realized that she had made it all the way to her enormous apartment complex without even noticing all the turns and stops along the way. Was it any wonder, she asked herself, as she pulled into the underground garage, out of the barrage of rain pelting Las Vegas for the first time in months? What happened when she got up to her tenth-floor apartment might be one of the most important turning points of her life. And there was no turning back now.

She unbuckled her seat belt, gathered up her purse, in which she'd tucked the bag from the pharmacy, and the paper bags of fresh bagels and cream cheese she'd used as her excuse to leave the house so early this morning, and stepped out of her car, swinging her hips to close the door behind her. Then she made her way to the elevator, stopping halfway to the doors when she remembered what she'd forgotten in the car. A bottle of sparkling cider, for a little toast if the news was indeed, as she hoped, worth celebrating. She rushed back for it and managed to secret it away in the bag that held the tubs of cream cheese, where she hoped he wouldn't notice it until she'd told him what was going on. Then back to the elevator and up, up toward home.

When the doors opened with a chime, Marissa stepped out

into the hallway and turned left, starting down the long corridor to her apartment with great purpose. She unlocked and flung open her door and bounded inside.

But from behind the armful of bags she carried, she caught sight of something that made her stop dead in her tracks. Down the long hallway, sitting on her living room sofa across from Khalid, was a man with the exact same coloring as his. The man had bronze skin, dark heavy brows, and a black mustache. His hair was covered in a kind of hood that bobbed every which way as he spoke animatedly, but otherwise his dress was entirely Western—a fine suit and tie that accentuated the man's strong build and made it impossible to guess his age. He seemed agitated, and his gestures were big and staccato, as if he were trying to convince Khalid of something, but Marissa couldn't make out the words from the entryway.

For a moment she had no idea what to do. Should she race into the living room and find out what was what? Or leave them their privacy? She'd never seen the man before, and she couldn't help but think there was something foreboding about the way he carried himself along with the large metal briefcase that sat beside him on the floor. Something very unusual was under way here. Before she could think twice, she advanced on them as noisily as she could, calling out, "Khalid, I'm home!"

"Marissa!" Khalid exclaimed when she burst into the living room, her arms still laden with bags. "You're back already?"

Marissa started. Was that a guilty tone in his voice underneath his surprise? "Of course I'm back already," she said, looking from him to the stranger and back. "I only had to run to the bakery." Why did she sound so defensive? She chided herself for her unwelcoming behavior. This was not how she wanted to start such an important day.

Khalid lowered his chin slightly, and Marissa was taken, as she always was, by his beautiful shock of mahogany hair. "Of course, of course," he said. "Let me take those bags." He took her bundles and whisked them to a side table. Then he pulled her to him. "Marissa, I'd like you to meet Abdul-Malik Abbasi."

"Abbasi?" Marissa searched her brain as she shook the stranger's hand, trying to remember where she'd heard the name before. "Why does that sound so familiar?"

Khalid squeezed her to him tightly, and looked her right in the eyes, something that never failed to send chills up her spine. "Because," he whispered in his low voice , "it is the surname of the man who signed the 'father' box on my birth certificate."

Marissa gasped. She looked hard into the face of the man who stood in her living room, and took in his hooded eyes, the strong, broad nose on his face, and that razor-cut jaw that looked so similar to Khalid's. She did see a remarkable resemblance, but now that she was facing him straight on, this man seemed far too old to be Khalid's father. "Are you saying he's related to you?" she whispered back, trying to avoid being out-and-out rude.

But he heard her perfectly, and crossed the room in long strides to shake her hand. "Ms. Madden, I presume?" he asked in a thick accent.

"Yes, but how did you know that?" she asked brazenly, all thought of decorum out the window.

"My investigator tells me you are the woman in Khalid's life."

Not just any woman, but possibly the mother of his child, Marissa thought, but she bit her tongue. This was certainly not the time for that revelation. "Why would you have us investigated?" she asked him, her confusion—and trepidation—rising.

"I apologize for the intrusion on your privacy. As I explained to Khalid earlier, I had you investigated because I was looking for my grandson," the older man said matter-of-factly. "And now that I have found him, I promise I will scrutinize you no further."

Marissa let her gaze move back to Khalid, and saw from the lack of surprise on his face that he'd heard this already. But to her, it made no sense. "Khalid is adopted," she said, flustered. "He grew up in the Nevada foster care system. He has no father, much less a grandfather."

The stranger—could he really be Khalid's grandfather?—shook his head slowly, a sad look on his face. "Though it shames me to no end to say so now that I know the truth, Khalid's father was my son. A troubled man, there can be no doubt, but to think that he abandoned his child for others to raise?" He crumpled his hand into a fist, as though he could bully the past into changing. Then he shrugged his shoulders, as if with just one motion he could put it all behind him. "It is regrettable. And it is more regrettable still that he is not alive today to explain himself. But in the end, he endeavored to make it right. For when he died—" With those words, the man put a hand to his chest, as if the hurt of his son's passing was still fresh. "—he left behind word of your existence. His last act, and a wise one too, was to ensure that the emirate exclave of Rifaisa would have an heir, and you, Khalid Abbasi, are that heir."

Marissa felt the color go out of her face at his words. They seemed perfectly crazy to her. An exclave? An emirate? An heir? But how could any of this be true? She thought back to the stories Khalid had told her early in their relationship. He was an orphan, raised in a succession of foster homes until age twelve, when a kind older couple legally adopted him and raised him as their own. He'd worked his way through college, and then gotten a great job that included school incentives that had allowed him to return to get his master's in business at night. It was a lot of living for a man only thirty-one years old, but nowhere in there had he mentioned anything about being the heir to an exclave in the Middle East.

She was pretty sure she would have remembered that little detail.

"Mr. Abbasi," Marissa started, since Khalid was silent. "This is all a very nice story, but surely you have Khalid mistaken for someone else?"

"There is no mistake, I assure you. I took great pains to be sure about what I'm telling you long before I darkened your doorstep. Let me show you." With his words, the man propped his shiny metal briefcase up on the back of the sofa, where Marissa and Khalid so often curled up together at the end of a long day. He put in the key codes and snapped the latches open, and retrieved an unlabeled manila envelope. Marissa watched wordlessly as he closed his briefcase just as methodically as he'd opened it, and then opened the envelope. He retrieved from within several sheets of paper and glossy photographs. It was obvious from only the slightest glimpse that the photos were of Khalid—taken by Abbasi's investigator, no doubt.

How long had this man been looking into them? Marissa wondered with a chill. But before she could ask, he handed Khalid a sheet of thick vellum for his inspection.

Khalid looked down at the sheet for a few moments and then back at Mr. Abbasi with a nod. "Show it to her, please," he said, and Marissa found herself wondering just how long this man had been talking to Khalid. He handed her the papers, and she glanced down at them, took in the seal from one of Las Vegas's most prominent medical centers.

"You had Khalid's DNA tested?" Pushed too far, her voice was defiant, angry.

"Please understand," the older man said, his hands open wide. "Rifaisa may be small, but it is still a very wealthy state, and the sheikh who rules it all, rich beyond words. I had to be absolutely sure that your Khalid was the true heir, or a disastrous mistake could have been made."

"But how?" Marissa interjected.

"It is frighteningly easy," he said with a dismissive wave. "A discarded cup of coffee, or clippings of hair from the barber."

Khalid shook his head. "It is almost more than can be believed," he said to Marissa, "but what he says appears to be true."

Mr. Abbasi gave one slow nod. "It is unbelievable news," he said, taking a sideways step closer to Khalid. "But it is also joyous news for the kingdom of Rifaisa. The people have long prayed for a strong leader who can take the reins of power when my time is at an end. My son, sadly, was not up for the task. But I can see with my own eyes that my grandson is truly worthy." As he spoke, Marissa saw him move a hand quickly up to his eye, but not quick enough. One fat tear escaped down his cheek.

Khalid's eyes seemed bright as well, she noticed, and it made her heart bend to see it. What must he be feeling right now? To think, for his entire life, he was alone, without family, discarded. But then to discover, all in one fateful morning, that he was part of a grand line of royalty? If Marissa didn't know Khalid so well, she might have found it unbelievable. But it wasn't hard to believe he was of royal blood. His broad shoulders and heavy brows, the powerful way he moved through life, his decisive manner—there was no question in her mind now that he was born to rule.

But where did that leave her? Or the unborn baby that might be growing this very second within her?

"Khalid," the older man said, his voice firmer, as if he could somehow stifle the emotion bubbling within him with strength. "I know this must all come as quite a shock. But as I was telling you before Marissa arrived, there is no time to come to terms with the news. The time has come for you to step up to the responsibilities you were born into. Rifaisa cannot go another moment without knowing of your existence. The news will bring much-needed optimism for the future and quiet the factions who would scrabble for power when I am gone." He clapped one tanned hand on Khalid's powerful shoulder. "Grandson, it is time for you to come home at last."

"Home," Khalid repeated, and Marissa saw in his eyes a look of such longing it nearly made her heart break.

All her life she'd had her family, all those brothers within reach whenever she needed them. For the first time in his life,

Khalid was being offered that same blessing. She could hardly ask him not to grab it with both hands.

Mr. Abbasi smiled. "Yes, home. My jet is waiting at the airport. You and I will be on our way to Rifaisa by noon today."

Marissa's heart clutched. "Noon!" she cried. "But I. We." She hardly knew how to protest.

"He'll be back," the older man said, his voice now a soothing balm. "It will only be a month, maybe two. He'll merely come, get acquainted with the kingdom and his family—and his duties—and then he can decide where to live, and who to bring into his new life."

There was something about the way he worded that last bit that made Marissa terribly uncomfortable, but she stifled her fears. Khalid would come back for her; of course he would. It was impossible to doubt the love they shared.

Khalid once again took her by the hand, and then moved around to take her other hand in his and lock his eyes with hers. She searched his dark eyes for answers. Was this what he wanted? Would he come back for her? His eyes seemed so confident, so warm, almost glittering with excitement. Even knowing he was suddenly a powerful sheikh, he seemed the same devastatingly handsome man she'd fallen in love with a year ago. The man who'd made her wildest dreams come true by telling her he loved her back.

"Grandfather," Khalid said, not removing his gaze from hers. "We need a moment of privacy, if you don't mind."

"Of course," the older man said, and he moved into the hallway and closed the door behind him.

When they were alone, Khalid ran one hand through Marissa's curly brown hair, pushing a lock that had fallen over her eyes back behind her ear, letting his hand linger on her face when he was done. "Beautiful girl," he whispered. "I hardly know what to say."

Say you'll stay here with me! Marissa thought for a moment, but she shook those thoughts away. It would be too selfish to ask such a thing of him. "Say you'll come back for me," she said at last, letting two tears escape from her eyes.

"I'll come back for you," he said, his voice thick and low. "But I have to go. I have to see what this is all about. All my life I've wanted to know who I came from—where I belonged. This is my chance."

"Of course," Marissa said, but inside she was warring with herself. Should she tell him about the pregnancy test now? What if he left, went halfway across the world, and she discovered she was pregnant? How would she break the news? On the phone?

But what if it was all a false alarm? Telling him she might be pregnant now would turn his world upside down, when it was already spinning off its axis almost uncontrollably. No. She would wait until she knew for sure. Then she could tell him in person, when he came back. The thought of it gave her a thrill. She imagined him returning to Las Vegas a newly made sheikh, taking her in his arms. And then she would tell him the exciting news that they were soon going to welcome another member of the Abbasi line.

The fantasy gave her a secret smile. She used it to look into his eyes and let him go, as she knew she must. "Go, Khalid," she said, working to hold her voice steady. "I will miss you with all my heart, but the world is small these days. We can text, and call, and videochat whenever we want. And before we know it, you'll be ready to return to me." She tipped up her head to him, and he bowed his down and captured her lips in a searing kiss that reminded her how incredibly precious their love was.

"Thank you, beautiful girl," he said, when their lips at last parted. "I love you, forever." And then he gave her another kiss and held her tight for a slow, quiet moment, and then with one last long look, he picked up the bag he always brought with him to her apartment, with his laptop and cell phone tucked away inside, and then he was gone.

When the door closed behind him, Marissa sank to the hardwood floor, feeling suddenly exhausted, as if she'd run a marathon, and not simply kissed Khalid goodbye. He would be back, she reminded herself once, then again and again, until she realized she was weeping. Had she made the right choice not to tell him what she suspected? Yes, she decided with finality. He had already had so much shock today. Adding this to the list would only make it harder for him to do what he had to do—go to Rifaisa and learn where he came from. If he thought she were pregnant, he would have insisted on staying, and that would forever be on her conscience. She'd done what was best for Khalid.

But what was best for her?

Gathering her strength, Marissa stood, and crossed to the counter where she'd left her purse only a few minutes ago—though it felt like a lifetime. Inside, the pregnancy test was waiting in its soft pink box with the illustration of the words "Yes" and "No" in white bubbles across the front. She slipped the test from her purse and looked at it for a long time, debating whether she should take it now or wait until the shock of this morning's events had worn off. But she couldn't wait another moment. She was dying to know. So she removed the plastic covering on the box and opened it up, removing one packet wrapped in white paper. The instructions were simple, printed in friendly icons across the top of the packet. Two minutes, said the label. In two minutes' time, she'd know if she was carrying the son or daughter of a sheikh.

She rolled her lips together, thinking again of telling Khalid the good news. In her mind's eye, she was picking him up at the airport, standing on the tarmac, not caring about the gusts of wind around them or the noisy thunder of the jet engines in every direction. She would kiss him, and then rise up on her tiptoes so she could whisper the news in his ear. "We're pregnant," she would say, and then he would pick her up and spin her around and they would both cry with joy. Marissa closed her eyes for a moment, picturing it in such detail that she thought for a moment she could make it real.

But when she opened her eyes, she was still standing in her tenth-floor apartment, clutching the pregnancy test like her life depended on it. And Khalid was still gone. So she took a deep breath, dried her tears, and walked straight into the bathroom, ready to find out the truth.

1

CAIRO, THREE YEARS LATER

THE FOUR SEASONS HOTEL CAIRO WAS A BUSTLING PLACE, FULL OF energy and life and sights so beautiful they seemed almost unreal. On one side of the building, picture windows draped with lush embroidered curtains displayed magnificent views of the famous Nile River, where the city lights of Cairo danced off the surface of the water and suggested a magical quality to the place worthy of all of the legends. On the other side, a verdant sea of trees, and far off on the horizon, the pointed tips of the pyramids, jutting over the tops of the leaves. The view took Marissa's breath away. Never in her life had she seen such amazing sights—and all in one place. Though she missed her family already, she wished that the conference she was attending here would last three weeks instead of just the three days that were scheduled. She could spend at least that long exploring this amazing city.

But she was here with a purpose, she reminded herself. Ever since she'd been promoted to marketing manager of her brother's wildly successful contracting company a year and a half before, she'd been constantly busy with the demands of the job. And that was a good thing—it took her mind off of the heartbreak that had chased her around for almost three years, leaving it hard for her to sit still for even a moment without being overcome by regret and sadness.

But sitting still in Cairo certainly wouldn't be an issue. There was so much to do here, and on top of all of the things she wanted to see, there were several important meetings at the conference that could net Madden Construction a fortune. There was no question of her mission here.

But first, Marissa thought with a sigh, she needed a long, hot shower. The trip from Las Vegas had been an exhausting one, with a long layover in New York and then an overnight flight that had left her completely disoriented. She looked at her watch for the tenth time in as many minutes, reminding herself that though it felt like early morning, it was actually just after noon, and time for lunch. The thought of eating seemed impossible, but she knew the best way to get over jet lag was through regular meals. Her shower would have to wait just a little longer.

With a sigh, she checked in, asking that her bags be sent up to her room ahead of her and retrieving a book to read over lunch first. Then she made her way to the lushly appointed restaurant, checking herself out in one of the full-length mirrors that flanked the elevators, reflecting the enormous floral displays over and over again and making the halls seem even larger than they were. Her traveling clothes had served her well, she thought. The long black trousers and topaz blue tunic she'd changed into near the end of the flight were only slightly creased, and she'd tied up her dark brown curls in a low, loose ponytail, with a silk scarf serving as a headband to keep the unruliest hairs in place. All told, she looked very presentable for someone who'd been traveling since time began, she decided with some satisfaction. Certainly nice enough for a quick lunch, even at the Four Seasons.

The hostess at the restaurant was gracious, and seated her at a distant, quiet table right by one of the enormous windows, so that she could watch the Nile trickle by slowly just a few feet from where she ate. Smoked salmon and fresh fruit squeezed with lemon and drizzled in yogurt were the closest things to breakfast food she could think to order, but when they came, she found room in her stomach for only a few bites before resting her fork on the edge of the large plate and focusing on a soothing cup of tea. She was lost in her book, planning to try again with her food after a moment's respite, when she stopped, mid-sentence, feeling a sudden urge to look up and around.

When she did, her breath was taken away by a sight even more disarming than the one out the window.

"Khalid," she whispered softly to herself. It was as if she'd felt his presence the moment he'd walked into the dining room. Dressed in an immaculate business suit and dark crimson tie, he stood perhaps thirty feet away, by the hostess stand, lost in conversation with a shorter, less interesting man whom Marissa didn't recognize. Undetected, she stared openly at the man she'd once loved more than life itself. A man she hadn't seen in three long years.

Time had changed Khalid little. He still took up more space in the room than any man had the right to, with his broad shoulders, strong chest, and a stance that spoke of power and confidence. And he still had the shock of dark, dark hair that she had so loved running her fingers through. But on his face there were new lines near his eyes—the creases, she suspected, of duty and responsibility. She knew from her favorite news websites that he was the royal heir to the tiny exclave of Rifaisa, with its shipping port that housed every oil tanker making its way from the Middle East to Europe at least once in both directions. No doubt, his obligation was a large one. Surely he was a very busy man.

He'd certainly been too busy for her, she thought with a pang. At first, when he'd left her to visit Rifaisa and meet his biological family, they'd texted and talked on the phone every day. But within a few weeks, the emails had slowed, and after two months, the calls grew rarer and rarer still. He'd become so engrossed in his new life as a sheikh that he'd found less and less time for

Marissa. Surely, she imagined, her little life in America would have seemed so boring and pedestrian to him, the more he learned of his noble birthright. But still, she had believed he would come back for her as soon as he was able to get away.

And then, after three months of separation, the accident. Just the merest thought of that time nearly brought tears to her eyes. She'd been devastated, unable to talk to anyone. Even Khalid. She'd hidden away in her parents' home, speaking to no one, hardly able to even eat for months and months.

When the grief had finally worn off enough for her to face the outside world, it was too late. The news had been all over the Web, even in a few of the tabloids. Pictures of the opulent wedding had been featured in *The New York Times.*

Marissa looked around, scanning the restaurant, hoping the hurt and heartbreak didn't read on her face. *Where was Khalid's new wife?* she wondered. Was she here, in this very room, within shouting distance of the woman he'd left alone in America? The dining room was full, but Marissa saw no one who met her description—glamorous, beautiful, mysterious—and brought her eyes back to Khalid.

And found, when she did, that he was staring intently right back at her.

WHEN KHALID ABBASI laid eyes on Marissa Madden, sitting in front of a beautiful view of the lazy Nile, his first emotion was anger. *How dare she come here, to his side of the world,* he thought— until he realized the foolishness of such a sentiment and scolded himself. Cairo was hundreds of miles from Rifaisa, and there was no way she could have known he'd be here today. Even some of his closest advisors didn't know he was here. He'd told them he was going to spend some quiet time with his ailing grandfather. But Abdul-Malik knew Khalid was really in Cairo, trying to broker a very tenuous trade agreement with a pair of brothers, sheikhs from a landlocked area near Rifaisa, a place that needed port access but had a history of contentious relationships with the leaders of Khalid's land. A deal was by no means a sure thing, but if he was successful, it could mean a huge increase in port tax revenues for Rifaisa, and in turn, more prosperity for his people. He couldn't let news of it leak to the media and chance raising the hopes of the entire country without justification.

Even so, it was an important deal, and there was no one on earth he was less happy to see here than Marissa. The very sight of her threatened his composure, risked his focus. She looked as beautiful as ever. When her large, blue-green eyes locked with his, her full lips parted slightly in surprise. He remembered drawing his fingers over that face, stroking her lips softly, kissing each of her eyelids, and then leaving a trail of kisses down her face at night, before they fell asleep. The memory left a bitter taste in his mouth.

There was nothing for it. He'd have to go over there, greet her, make nice, and be done with it. Tomorrow he would be gone from here and never have to see her—or think of her betrayal—again. He squared his shoulders and headed straight for her table, not noticing as he walked away from one of his advisors mid-sentence.

It took just a few moments to cross the room with his long strides, and he did not break eye contact with her the entire time. She too, kept her eyes steady, looking down for only a moment right as he appeared at her table.

"Khalid," she said, her voice quieter, more unsure than he remembered it.

"Good afternoon, Marissa. It's such a surprise to see you here in Cairo."

She swallowed. "And you, as well. Are you here on business?" she asked.

"Of course," he said dismissively. He had little time for anything but state business these days. "And you?"

"A conference," she said, her chin raising slightly as she spoke, a habit he had found so endearing way back when. "For Madden Construction."

"You work for your brother now?" he asked.

"Yes. Ever since..." her voice trailed off. "It's been about two and a half years. I'm Knox's marketing manager."

Khalid exhaled slowly. "I see. The company is doing well, then?"

Marissa nodded slightly, not breaking eye contact. "Very well, thank you. Still growing, albeit cautiously in this economic environment. I'm meeting with a few potential new accounts here."

"Will you be in Cairo long?" he asked, wishing he didn't care so much about her answer, wondering how she still managed to affect him so.

"Just three days," she said, a wistful tone in her voice. "It's such a beautiful city. I wish I had longer to see all the sights."

Khalid scoffed. "I'm sure there will be no shortage of men lining up to show you around." He hoped she understood his cold tone.

"Maybe," Marissa said slowly, her eyes looking upward as if she were thinking of something. Then she added, more to herself than him, "But none of them are you."

The words took him aback. That she could pretend to still care for him, even after her betrayal, irked him to no end. "What do you mean by that?" he demanded.

"Nothing," she said quickly, with a dismissive wave. "Forget I said it."

"I wish I could forget everything you ever said to me," he said darkly. "All the promises we made." He stopped himself before he gave away how badly she'd hurt him.

Marissa looked down, shamed no doubt by her behavior.

Good. Then she angled her face upwards and said, softly again, "That's all in the past, right?"

Khalid nodded, satisfied. "All in the past."

For a moment, neither of them spoke, just took each other in. Then he saw Marissa's shoulders rise and fall—a deep breath—and she parted her lips to speak. "Maybe this—us running into each other—is a blessing in disguise," she began. "We haven't spoken in more than two years. Perhaps we should sit down, talk some things out."

"Why would I want to do a thing like that?" Khalid asked harshly.

"Because," Marissa replied quickly, her voice strong and resolute now, reminding him of how, when she really wanted something, when it was truly important to her, there was no use in denying her. "Because there are some things I need to tell you. Things I should have told you a long time ago. And I need the closure."

Khalid felt his hands ball into fists. She thought she deserved closure? After what she had done the moment his back was turned? He thought the scowl on his face would be all the answer she needed, but then she took him by surprise. Reached out her hand for his wrist, and gently held him there, imploring.

"Please, Khalid," was all she said, but he felt his resolve melt. The look on her face, one of regret mixed with beseeching, was exactly the same look that had been on her face when she'd sent him to Rifaisa all those years ago. At the time, he'd thought she'd parted with him so willingly because it was what was best for him. It was months before he'd realized the real reason she'd sent him away without a second thought.

Because she was in love with another man.

Well, then, Khalid reasoned. Let her talk to him. Tell him the truth she'd been hiding for so long. His heart was disconnected from hers now. She could cause him no further pain. He doubted anyone could.

"Fine," he said, making sure his resistance was clear. "We'll dine tonight, in my suites. Eight o'clock. I'll have someone meet you in the lobby and take you where you need to go."

"But," Marissa protested, "wouldn't it be better if we met on more neutral ground?"

"Perhaps it would be better for you. But I have a closely regimented schedule now. And I'll need to be where I've said I'll be to avoid giving my staff a security nightmare."

Marissa looked around, perhaps noticing for the first time the guards stationed in three places through the room, watching them intently. "Of course," she said after a moment. "Eight o'clock. I'll see you then."

Khalid looked deep into those blue-green eyes of hers, trying to get a feel for what emotion lay within them. She'd always been hard to read, her smooth surface rarely giving away much. But, he remembered, when she'd been overjoyed, her eyes had seemed to shimmer, as though the happiness was flowing right through her body and pouring out of them. Now, they were glassy and blank and told him nothing.

He hoped he was as inscrutable to her, he thought, as he turned and stalked out of the cavernous dining room, eager to put the past—at least as it applied to Marissa Madden—far behind him.

WALKING into her luxury hotel room for the first time should have been a dazzling enough experience to take Marissa's mind off of her encounter with Khalid. But despite the sweeping views of downtown Cairo and the beautifully decorated space, with its plush all-white bedding and sleek cherrywood furniture, her thoughts never left the sight of Khalid's face standing next to her table, scowling at her.

She'd been so surprised by his reaction to her. She thought at best he'd be happy to see her—at worst, their meeting would be a reminder of a time before he was the powerful leader he was today. But instead he'd seemed almost angry. His brusque tone and lack of patience for her made her wonder if he was holding resentments against her. But that would make no sense. He was the one who'd left her alone in the States, waiting and hoping he'd come back.

So that she could tell him she was carrying his child.

Eager to distract herself, Marissa kicked off her shoes and went to check out the bathroom. A huge, glass-encased shower promised enough hot water and steam to wipe her brain clean of old hurts, so she slipped off her clothes and turned on the water. Once she was inside, the thick streams of water served their purpose, reinvigorating her, clearing away the film of travel. By the time she was finished, she felt so much better that she was convinced dinner tonight with Khalid *was* a good idea. She'd meet with him, break bread, and tell him about everything that had happened after he'd left. Then she'd get on with her business here and return home with a fresh outlook on her life. She'd finally close the chapter on Khalid.

Even after the shower and preparing for her first meeting of the conference, she still had thirty minutes to herself. So she quickly booted up her computer. Within seconds, she was video-chatting with one of her best friends back in Las Vegas.

"Well, well," said a man's voice through her tinny laptop speakers, before the face on the screen even came up.

"Grant, is that you? I don't have picture yet, but you sure don't sound like Jenna."

The man laughed, and then his smiling face at last appeared. "That's a good thing," said Grant. "I'd hate to think my phone voice could be mistaken for my wife's."

"I've got picture now," said Marissa. "And wow! Is that a Vegas Golden Knights jersey behind you? Have you been making jewelry for the jocks again?" Owning jewelry made by Grant

Blakely's jewelry empire had become a favorite status symbol for their hometown hockey heroes—and the players' girlfriends.

"You better believe it. Remember Brad Bradley, the sports agent that went to B-school with us? He keeps name dropping McCormick Diamonds to his clients. And did Knox tell you? We got together on a box for the Knights' inaugural season in Vegas."

Marissa shook her head and laughed. "Score one more for that Notre Dame MBA," she said jokingly. "Just see that you boys don't work too hard."

"Hey, one does what one can when their job doesn't send them on an all-expenses-paid trip to see the pyramids," Grant teased. "How's Cairo?"

"So far, eventful," she said, knowing there was no point in hiding her news from him. Marissa had been close with Grant's wife, Jenna, ever since Jenna met Grant. And they'd just gotten closer when an SUV had crossed the highway median and hit the car Grant and Marissa were traveling in head-on.

They'd been driving to Grant's office that day to collaborate on an engagement ring for Jenna. With Marissa's help, Grant had planned a romantic proposal, complete with Champagne and flowers, and all he'd needed was a ring he was sure Jenna would love. But in the end, *Jenna* had proposed to *Grant* in his hospital bed, where he'd been relegated after the accident with two bruised ribs.

While Marissa had recovered two floors away from an injury far more severe.

"What do you mean, eventful?" Grant asked, leaning his face closer into the computer screen, as if he could somehow read deeper into Marissa's eyes, over the thousands of miles and millions of electrons that separated them. "What's going on?"

"I saw Khalid," she said. "He's here, in the same hotel."

Grant's jaw dropped. "In Cairo at the same time as you? What are the chances?"

"I know," Marissa said, shaking her head. "But maybe it's a

good thing, Grant." She hoped she sounded more confident than she felt. "This may be a chance at the closure I've always needed."

Grant pulled his head back, surprised. "Are you saying you're going to tell him about the baby?"

Marissa sighed. "I think so. It just feels like the right thing to do."

Grant was quiet for a moment. "Are you sure, Mari?" he asked, using the nickname he'd borrowed from Jenna long ago. "That could bring up a lot of long-buried pain for you."

She shook her head adamantly now. "Nothing is buried. I realized that the moment I laid eyes on him. It was as if the whole horrible thing had just happened days ago. It all came rushing back."

"Losing your baby at 24 weeks has to be traumatic," Grant said. "It's normal for old memories to surface from time to time and feel just as powerful as ever. But they'll fade, if you give them a chance."

"Don't you turn philosophical on me, Grant Blakely. You were there when it happened. You remember the accident as clearly as I do."

"Of course I do," he said softly. "If there were some way to go back and change that day, it would be the first thing I'd do. I know how much you were looking forward to being a mother."

"And you know how strongly I believed that Khalid would be a wonderful father," she said. "And he deserves to know about the daughter he lost that day. She was a part of him, too, even if he doesn't know it."

"I'm not sure what he deserves, given how he abandoned you."

Marissa smiled wanly into her webcam. "I know you love to protect me, but let's face facts. He didn't so much abandon me as become a different person. With a different life. Far removed from the life we'd had together."

"A different life, complete with a new wife," Grant added

bitterly. "Look. Jenna and I want you to be happy. If you think this will bring you closure, I can't stop you from going for it. But be careful, and never forget how he hurt you."

She nodded solemnly. "I promise I won't forget. But maybe I can forgive." Then she looked at her watch. "Okay, it's time for me to jet. I've got a meeting in five downstairs, and after that I have three hours free, so I'm going to hit the Egyptian Museum and try not to think about Khalid the entire time. Wish me luck!"

"Good luck. Jenna will be back in a couple hours. I'll catch her up then."

"Send her my love!" Marissa closed the browser window, grabbed her purse, and launched herself through the door, ready to forget her recent past. Ancient Egyptian history seemed a lot more manageable today.

2

THREE YEARS AGO, WHEN KHALID HAD FIRST ARRIVED IN RIFAISA, they'd called him the Son of the Prodigal Son. Funny, since he'd never gotten to meet his father, that it was his father's reputation that stuck in the minds of the Rifaisi people.

But that misconception hadn't lasted long. Soon enough, the whispers shifted, declaring how different he was from his father. After all, within just a few months Khalid had learned enough about the history and government of his new home to best many a native historian, and he'd stepped up to the job of assisting his grandfather in the exclave's leadership with admirable competency. Where his father had been known for his interest only in the perks of a royal life, Khalid, if anything, erred on the side of being too serious for the tastes of his people. Over the years, his grandfather's press secretary had spent hours with him, coaching him to appear less "stiff," as she was in a habit of describing him. As his grandfather's health declined, and it became clear that his retirement was closer than either of them had ever imagined, Khalid's public image grew more and more important. As his advisors were constantly reminding him, Rifaisa deserved not just to respect their nation's leader, but also to like him.

The sentiment drove Khalid to distraction. Wasn't it enough that he had taken over so many of his grandfather's duties—jobs Abdul-Malik had had a lifetime to learn and master—in just under three years, since his true identity had been discovered? Would they have preferred his father, a man so wrapped up in himself that he'd abandoned his own son as soon as the burdens of parenthood had begun to take time away from his social life?

He sighed and pushed himself out of the chaise he had been sitting on, turned his view away from the pyramids outside his suite's windows to the large room where he waited for his next visitor to arrive. Near the door, his chief assistant glanced at his watch, then flipped his wrist over to type something into his phone. At the dining table, which was in use as a conference table at the moment, two advisors sat scrutinizing a stack of contracts. Since discovering his true identity, Khalid had gotten used to being surrounded by people at all times. But every now and then, usually when he was preoccupied with thoughts of what he'd left behind in the United States, he felt the old familiar irritation he'd first struggled with at his lack of privacy.

At a time like this, when he was drowning in memories of *her*, he wished nothing more than to be alone.

"Leave me, please, Amid, Jana, Mostafa," He spoke in smooth Arabic to the two men and one woman who crowded his suite. "I must phone my grandfather."

Without so much as a word, his staff rose from their positions and moved out of the suite, leaving him alone in the vast space of the living room. Buried as he was in his thoughts, even the enormous room, full of perfectly styled furniture groupings and the various flotsam interior decorators loved so much, felt too claustrophobic for him. He brushed through the dining alcove and onto the balcony without a second thought for his phone, which lay untouched on a glass curio table inside. He'd called his grandfather already earlier that day, as his staff well knew. He'd simply used the only acceptable excuse for privacy.

Outside, the warm, windy air and expansive view of Egypt's beautiful landmarks instantly served as a balm on his ragged nerves. The sight of the botanical gardens in the foreground were a happy reminder of the royal gardens he took so much comfort in back home in Rifaisa. And the pyramids peeking out in the background, so magnificent and mysterious, were one of the few sights that could rival the sparkling blue Gulf of Oman he looked out on from his bedroom in the palace. Soon, he reminded himself, this deal would be done or lost, and either way he'd go back home and life would return to precision and order. Soon, Marissa Madden would go back to the past, where she belonged.

But first she wanted closure, he remembered with a groan. Perhaps what she was after was a chance to confess. Or maybe she would continue to pretend she'd never done anything untoward, as she had right up until she'd stopped returning his calls and letters, just three months after he left. At first he'd told himself there was some reason for her neglect. Perhaps, as his grandfather had suggested, she was angry with him because he was unable to return to the States as quickly as he'd first hoped. But that had been totally out of his control, as he'd explained in a series of unreturned emails. Processes had moved more slowly in Rifaisa than he'd anticipated. And political issues had required him to show his commitment to his new country. Rushing back to America would have spelled great doubt and upheaval. More upheaval, he feared, than his small exclave could handle.

Now, happily, conditions were much more stable, in large part because of the steadying influence that Khalid himself had had on matters of state. With a clear heir in place, the exclave was again ready to plan for the future, and they trusted Khalid to take them there.

But three years ago, leaving would have been too great a chance to take. Marissa should have understood that. Clearly, her attentions were elsewhere.

As he discovered when, after five months in Rifaisa, he scheduled a trip to Las Vegas. By then, Marissa had been uncommunicative for so long that he'd felt he had no other choice but to go to her in person, no matter the cost to the political situation in Rifaisa. But when, during his layover in Chicago, he'd seen Marissa's face on the cover of a trashy tabloid magazine, he'd stopped in his tracks. Inside, in a small sidebar story, was the scintillating tale of how McCormick Diamond's CEO Grant Blakely was on the prowl again. The notorious playboy, the story went on to report, had been in a car accident with his new girlfriend, Marissa Madden, en route to a planned shopping spree at his famous jewelry company.

First, Khalid had panicked. His Marissa was in a car accident! But after he'd ascertained from friends in Las Vegas that her injuries had been not at all life-threatening, he'd gotten the seedier details. Grant was a notorious Vegas playboy he'd met at a few business events long ago, and a friend of Marissa's brother Knox. He always had a new woman on his arm. But not long before the accident, he had abruptly disappeared from the Vegas nightlife scene. That disappearance had coincided to the day, not coincidentally, with Khalid's trip to Rifaisa.

Apparently, since his departure, Blakely had neatly filled in Khalid's place in Marissa's life. Sure enough, Khalid discovered with a simple phone call, the jewelry company's main suppliers had just shipped them several high quality diamonds for their consideration. All were stones meant for an extravagant engagement ring.

The realization was humiliating: Marissa wasn't answering her phone anymore because she was too busy enjoying her new, high-flying lifestyle—not, as Khalid had let himself imagine, because she was trying to force him to return to her. She'd moved on, and with a great deal of relish, too.

Meanwhile, he'd been doing his duty to his new homeland, thinking of her each day and night, counting the minutes until he could see her again.

Coming back to the present with a start, Khalid realized he was gripping the iron railing of his balcony with enough force to make veins stand out on his hands. His teeth were gritted, and the beautiful view before him had faded from his sight, replaced instead by the vision of that crowded, noisy Chicago airport where he'd put all the pieces together. That day had been one of the darkest in his life. Until then he'd never thought a woman like Marissa—so seemingly clear-eyed and optimistic no matter what life handed her—could be capable of such a betrayal. Now he knew the truth. Just as his father had abandoned him at the first sign of an obstacle, so too had the only woman he'd ever loved.

Khalid pushed a long dark strand of hair out of his eyes and forced himself to release his hold on the railing and turn back toward his suite. By now his staff would be in full gossip mode, whispering to each other about their stern boss, and his constant —and curious—demands for privacy. Or perhaps they'd have already heard from his security personnel of how he'd been in a heated conversation with an American woman in the hotel dining room. He could practically hear their exaggerated expressions of surprise at the news. "Sheikh Abbasi? Affected by a woman? Impossible," he imagined them whispering. And it *was* impossible. Marissa Madden would not overturn his emotional apple cart again after all this time. Whether she wanted to see him tonight for absolution or simply to carry on with her deception, he did not care.

Though he wouldn't mind making the experience as hard on her as possible.

With a wicked smirk at the thought, he moved back inside,

through his suite, and stepped swiftly into the hall, where he found Jana and Amid looking surprised and guilty enough that he knew his speculations of gossip had been dead on. He pretended not to notice. "Thank you for the privacy," he said in his normal standoffish tone. "If you'll step inside, I need to discuss my plans for this evening with you."

He waved them in and they followed like ducklings. Once he'd closed the door behind them, he gestured around the suite. "First things first. By tonight at eight p.m., I want there to be no trace of business left in this room."

Jana looked confused. "We're not working late tonight?" she asked, incredulous.

Khalid shook his head. "Quite the contrary. In fact, I'll need the suite to myself. After, of course, you've helped me set the stage...for a romantic dinner for two."

This time, he couldn't stop from smiling a little when he saw their looks of shock.

DINNERTIME CAME FAR TOO SOON for Marissa. Her meeting had gone brilliantly, and she'd paused in her hotel room afterward only long enough to send her brother-slash-boss a triumphant email before switching into much more comfortable flats and racing out again. She couldn't wait to see the famous Egyptian Museum, and she was not disappointed. Once she made it through the garden and inside, the crowded halls were full of people, and treasures were in every direction. It was a crush of the living and the long dead, the first marveling in what the second had left behind. Every direction she turned revealed a new host of wonders, from a stunning room of ancient mummies to a grand hall filled with sarcophagi and tombs. She'd lost the most time in a bright, hot room in the far corner of the second floor, where the possessions of Nefertiti were displayed. By the time she'd puzzled out the French labels in that hall, she'd realized she was covered with a fine coat of dust and sweat, as if she herself had been excavating the ruins. If she hoped to be at least remotely presentable for dinner—and in truth she wanted to look her very best, despite her common sense—she would need to hurry back to the hotel and start from scratch.

By the time she rushed out of her hotel room at five to eight that evening, Marissa felt like a new woman—on the outside. On the inside she felt as nervous as she'd felt on their first date, when Khalid had taken her to a little, out-of-the-way Italian restaurant with checkered tablecloths and Sinatra records playing nonstop. That dinner had turned out to be amazing—a date she'd never forget, not only because of their involved conversation and an unmistakable feeling of falling she'd had the moment he walked in. She also would never forget it because, in an attempt to keep from ending the evening, she'd ordered a double espresso after dessert, acting as though she were the sort of cosmopolitan woman who always drank that much caffeine at ten at night. Later, after he'd kissed her softly on the lips and bid her good-bye, she'd been so wired that instead of going to bed, she'd stayed up all night bouncing around the house, thinking endlessly of Khalid's sweet kiss and his dark eyes. And watching endless episodes of *Magnum, P.I.,* on cable. The next day at work she'd been half-asleep. To this day, when she tasted espresso she thought of Khalid—and Tom Selleck.

Down in the hotel lobby, she took a moment to check herself out in one of the full-length mirrors that seemed to grace every wall that wasn't already occupied by flowers or artwork. Her usually unruly brown curls were pinned up in an improvised French twist, and she wore what she hoped was the appropriate attire for a closure dinner: a sleeveless white picot blouse embellished with a long ruffle running down the button placket, and an embroidered cotton skirt that fell above her knee in a straight pencil cut. In the mirror she looked thinner than usual, and longer, too. The high-waisted skirt did wonders for her short-torso/long-legged frame, and the tan slingbacks she'd packed didn't hurt either. But neither did anything to hide the generous curve of her hips, she realized with a shrug. Khalid had always loved her curves, or so he'd said—and then he'd married a rail-thin woman. Maybe his tastes had changed, and he'd find her sizable caboose less appealing, she thought with a frown. Not that she cared what he thought of her anymore.

Before she could become too self-obsessed, she spotted a woman bee-lining toward her purposefully. Marissa took her in. She was tiny, swimming in a dark pantsuit with her black hair pulled back in a bun. She had the beautiful olive skin of the Rifaisi region, but she was certainly not Khalid's wife. That woman was more Amazon in appearance, or so she'd looked online.

"Ms. Madden?" asked the stranger hesitantly, in a thick accent.

"That's me." Marissa extended her hand. "Are you with Khalid?"

The woman looked taken back by Marissa's use of his first name, but took her hand gingerly and shook it regardless. "I'm Mr. Abbasi's assistant, yes. May I escort you to his suite, please?"

"Thank you," Marissa said warmly, following Khalid's assistant as she walked briskly to the nearest bank of elevators. "Please call me Marissa, by the way."

The woman frowned for a moment but then she shrugged ever so slightly, and a faint smile crossed her lips. "Very well. I'm Jana. Pleased to meet you."

"You too." Marissa was glad to see her companion's face relax a little. "How long have you worked for Mr. Abbasi?" She used his last name to keep Jana comfortable.

"Since the very beginning," Jana replied. "I worked at the palace before we even knew he existed. When we found out he was coming, I was given the honor of working on his team."

Marissa considered her wording. "I take it this was a very prestigious assignment?"

"Oh yes, very," Jana answered in her musical accent. "Everyone was so excited when the news broke. For years we'd thought that his grandfather, the sheikh, was the last of his line."

"What about Khalid's father?"

"He passed away just before Khalid arrived. But to be honest, Ms. Madden—Marissa"—Jana looked her in the eye as she spoke —"there wasn't ever much hope of him taking over the duties of the throne."

Marissa had figured out as much from what little Khalid had mentioned about his father in his early emails. But he'd never come out and said so, and it was interesting to have her suspicions confirmed. She nodded. "I see."

Before she could inquire further, the elevator doors chimed and slid open. "Here we are," said Jana, a smile in her voice. She gestured to the first door on the long hall, where a bodyguard nodded imperceptibly to them both and stepped to one side. "Presidential Suite," the door read.

Marissa gulped. For the first time, it occurred to her that she had an audience with royalty tonight. She looked to Jana to lead the way, but the aide didn't budge. "Will you be needing anything further?" Jana asked politely, already reaching for the buttons on the elevator.

"Thank you, no," Marissa said automatically, wondering if she should leap for the elevator door herself. But it was too late—she was here and the doors were sliding shut. She steeled herself and lifted a hand to knock.

She had to knock three times before Khalid appeared. When he did, Marissa wondered what on earth she'd been thinking to come to his hotel room in search of closure.

One look at him and she knew getting closure tonight was as likely as learning to fly. He wore a light-colored pair of linen trousers and a luxurious-looking cotton sweater in a heathered shade of oatmeal that made his brown skin seem to glow from within. His hair, the color of rich walnut and longer than it had been when they'd been together, was pushed back out of his eyes —still wet, as if he, too, had just rushed out of the shower. Without wanting to, she found herself picturing that shower, the water coursing over his tight, muscled body, beading on his skin, rolling down his strong back and slowing at his firm butt...

Stop! she told herself. *He's married.* Marissa exhaled and wondered when her imagination had gotten so wild. And then she remembered that the image wasn't imaginary at all. She'd seen it, the morning before he'd left, when she'd come into her little apartment bathroom to brush her teeth while he showered. She'd seen him there, wet and naked, and had wanted to step inside of the shower with him and kiss away the droplets as they fell. But she'd decided the pregnancy test was more important, so she'd just pecked him good-bye before going, leaning back to keep her shirt dry.

If she could go back in time, she knew in an instant, she wouldn't have cared about her shirt. She'd have taken the opportunity—every opportunity—to be in his arms again. To feel that body pressed up against hers. To lose herself in passion.

"Good evening, Marissa." Khalid's, low, rich voice brought her back to the moment. "You look lovely."

Marissa looked up at him, scrutinizing his features. The anger he'd shown her earlier was gone. In its place was something far more dangerous. Desire.

"Thank you." She swallowed hard. "And thank you for inviting me to dinner. I know it's awkward, seeing each other again after all these years. But I have to believe it's no coincidence that we'd run into each other so far from our homes."

"Oh no?" asked Khalid. "What is it then?"

"Opportunity," she replied. "A chance to put what happened behind us."

Khalid looked away from her for the first time since opening the door, and Marissa wondered if he was rolling his eyes at her.

He'd always been so matter-of-fact. He didn't believe in fate, or destiny, the way she did.

Or had, until she'd lost her baby.

"Come in," he said after a moment. "I hope you still enjoy seafood as much as you used to. I've asked the chef to do a few choices, but the main event is salmon."

"I do." Marissa was pleased that he'd remembered at least that much about her. "Very much, thank you." She stepped inside the grandly appointed suite and looked about her, taking in the delicious smells of dill and lemon floating through the room. She was in a sunken living room, full of sofas and wingback chairs, a few pointed towards an enormous flat-screen TV mounted on the wall above an understated gas fireplace that crackled quietly. To the left, a few steps led to a pair of French doors. They were closed, but the open curtains displayed a bedroom with a massive four-poster bed stacked high with silk pillows. Quickly, Marissa turned her head away. To the right was a bathroom, and straight ahead and up again was an alcove dining area nestled into a half-circle of bay windows. At closer examination, she saw that one of the windows was actually a door, opening to a balcony beyond. The balcony, she could guess, had an amazing view of the pyramids. Without a second thought she moved up the stairs to the dining room to get a better look.

"Hungry, are we?" asked Khalid, a smile creeping into his voice. "I'm glad I ordered so much food."

"No, it's not that," she said, turning back from the window to see him moving to join her. "It's the view. My room is on the Nile side of the building, which is beautiful. But these gardens, and the pyramids behind them. They're breathtaking."

Khalid reached her side and nodded. "They are indeed. If you enjoy that, you should make a point to visit the Egyptian Museum across the street, and see what was once inside those pyramids. There's so much to learn from a land this ancient."

Marissa turned from the view and smiled, happy to be relating to him so easily despite everything. "I've already been," she said excitedly. "But I saw only a small fraction of the collection. I could spend days in there. The history, and the beautiful art. Did you get to see the room with all of Nefertiti's gold artifacts?"

Khalid furrowed his brow. "Regrettably, I've never been able to spend more then five minutes there."

Marissa stopped her lips. "Oh," she said, feeling foolish.

He folded his hands together. "It's not from lack of interest. I come to Cairo every few months to do business, but I've yet to find any time to tour. My schedule is tight. It has been since the day I met my grandfather."

Marissa thought of his sporadic emails and calls as he grew more and more involved. "I know," she said. "I can't begin to imagine the demands of this—do I call it a job? Is being a royal a job?"

Khalid smiled slightly. "It most certainly is. A job that I never go home from," he said, sounding weary. "And an honor," he added quickly.

Marissa searched his face, wondering for the first time if he regretted taking on such a huge responsibility. She'd always assumed he'd been eager to take his place as a wealthy sheikh and leader. But now she saw that the job had taken its toll.

"Your life has changed so much since the last time I saw you," she said. "You used to enjoy your freedom so much."

"And you've changed as well," he said, moving back from her slightly, then covering up the movement by reaching to a side table for a bottle of Pinot Gris. "Wine?"

She nodded, confused by his comment, and he poured her a glass, but took none for himself. "You don't drink anymore?"

"Drinking isn't socially acceptable in Rifaisa," he said. "I have a glass of scotch from time to time, in private." He picked up a snifter she hadn't noticed, poured himself one finger of an amber liquid, and raised the glass to his full lips. "This is one of those times."

An uncomfortable silence built between them. After a moment, Marissa realized she had been staring at his mouth, where the glass had been seconds earlier. Unconsciously, she licked her own lips. Then she cleared her throat. "The wine is very good," she said, desperate for distraction.

"Is it?" he asked, one eyebrow raised. "You haven't tasted it yet."

She looked down at her glass. Sure enough, there was no trace of the telltale lipstick mark that she usually left on the lip of her stemware. She flushed. "It has nice legs," she said, parroting a phrase her wine-buff father was known to bandy about when a wine clung well to the inside of its vessel.

"I see. Legs." Khalid replied with a slight smirk, and then she watched as he ran his eyes up and down her legs, as if she herself were a glass of wine for him to swirl around and taste. Her mouth went dry, and she took a sip of the wine to cover her embarrassed gasp.

When she swallowed, she struck back. "Would your wife be happy to know I'm here with you, in your hotel suite right now?"

Khalid's eyes narrowed. "Perhaps we should sit down for dinner now. The food is on heating trays, but it won't hold forever."

Marissa frowned, but drifted to the chair he'd gestured toward. Before she'd made hardly a move to sit, he was there, pulling the chair out just as he'd done that night at the Italian restaurant. The gesture was tiny, but like a brick through glass it shattered the calm she'd gathered about her and brought back all the pain Khalid had ever caused her. *What was she doing here?* she asked herself. *Why was she in this man's suite when his wife was God knows where?*

She popped up in her chair and whirled around to face him. "I should go. It's not proper for me to be here with you alone. You're a married man, and we were lovers once. Think of how it would look." Khalid stood in her way like a concrete wall, but she tried to push past him nevertheless.

He raised his hands and grabbed her by the shoulders. "Relax, Marissa," he said, holding her still despite her struggle. "My wife doesn't care who I have dinner with. We've been divorced for almost two years."

3

Marissa stopped at once, her hands still on Khalid's chest to push him away, but her body froze in place. "You're divorced?" she said, unable to process what he'd just told her.

Not breaking eye contact, he nodded once, slowly. "The marriage was a sham. A publicity stunt gone wrong."

She shook her head, stepped back, and pulled her hands from his body, feeling the cold loss of their touch. "But why would you marry someone for publicity?" she asked, incredulous. Her mind was swimming with the news. For so long she'd believed he was lost to her forever. Now she felt the old ache dissolving. Could it be possible that they might have a second chance?

"I didn't. At least not on purpose. My grandfather arranged the marriage, when he saw that you and I were over. It was political in nature—she's the daughter of a very important sheikh —but I had no objection. The only woman I wanted was no longer an option."

Marissa flinched at that, hurt. He was, she figured, implying that a man of royalty such as himself couldn't possibly marry an American commoner. *Was that really true, in this day and age?*

Marissa wondered. But how could she possibly know what the people of Rifaisa would abide?

She sat back down slowly, realizing that if that were the case, there would be no second chance for them. She shouldn't have even let herself think it. "And then what happened?" she asked, curious despite herself.

"And then we were married, and I soon discovered that my new bride was after more than just title and honor. She wanted limitless resources and a life of leisure and fame. She had no interest in doing her political duties as my wife, and certainly not in risking her figure and freedom to produce an heir for the country." He shook his head angrily but did not move from where he stood at Marissa's side. "It was only a few weeks before we decided to dissolve the marriage, for both of our sakes. But we waited six months to announce it, for the sake of appearances." His face twisted. "That was time wasted. She was seen in public with another man just a few days after our divorce."

Marissa gasped at that. She couldn't imagine any woman getting over Khalid that quickly. His wife must have been truly coldhearted. "How shameless."

Khalid looked at her for a long moment, then turned and took his place across the table. "I'm surprised you, of all people, would think that," he said coldly as he draped his napkin over his lap.

She set her jaw, determined to hold on to her equilibrium. "I don't know what you mean by that. But I'm sorry that your marriage went so badly. Truly, I am. Even back then, I wanted you to be happy. That is why I let you go in the first place."

He snorted. "Let me go? That's an interesting way to put it."

Marissa held tightly to her composure. "I wanted you to be with your family," she said, insistently. "I knew how you'd longed to find out where you truly belonged. This was your one chance. I understood that, though it hurt. I wanted you to have what I have —a family you could always turn to, no matter what." She paused, then forced herself to say what she'd come here to tell him. "But don't think for a second that it didn't break my heart."

At that, Khalid locked eyes with her, and would not look away for a very long time, as if he were trying to see inside her, to read her mind. She thought of the way he'd always seemed to know what she was thinking back when they were together—how easy it had been for him to finish her sentences. Would he see through her just as easily now? See how much trouble she was having keeping her heart protected now that she was so near him again?

She shuddered and prayed not.

At last, Khalid broke his stare. He turned to the sideboard behind him and picked up a serving platter of bright pink salmon hunks tossed with preserved lemons, and another heaped with fluffy mashed potatoes. "Let's eat," he said, as if she hadn't just spilled her heart out in front of him. "There's a salad back here somewhere...ah. Strawberries, spinach, goat cheese, and mint," he announced, and then reached for the salad tongs to serve her. Marissa decided to follow his lead and let the subject drop. Perhaps, like her, he was also having trouble keeping composure amongst all these painful memories. After all, he'd been through a divorce, she reminded herself. He was a single man again.

"Thank you," she said, holding her plate up to make it easier for him to serve the vibrantly colored salad, pushing thoughts of his marital status out of her mind. "I must say, it can't be the norm to get a private dinner with a sheikh. What happened to all those bodyguards and aides I saw you with at lunch?"

Khalid's face bent into a slight frown, and he shook his head. "Believe me, I'm quite happy to have an excuse to be rid of them for the night. I'm sure their tongues are wagging about you and me, but it's well worth it to have a moment's privacy."

"I take it privacy is an uncommon resource in your new lifestyle?"

"Very."

Marissa took a bite of her salad and paused to savor the flavor of smooth cheese melding with mint and berries. It was heaven. When she swallowed, she asked, "I'm not getting you in trouble, then, am I?"

"Hardly. In fact, dismissing the staff for the evening is probably the best thing I could be doing for my image right now. I've been criticized for being too stern. Working too much. Apparently I'm not 'fun' enough for public opinion."

Marissa laughed at this. "Not fun enough! That can hardly be the case. Remember that night in Vegas when the temperature rose so high that it was too hot to sleep? How you took me to that country club pool at midnight and showed me how to climb the fence?"

A tiny smile broke out on Khalid's face, starting with a curve of the lips and then moving up to the wrinkles around his eyes. "How could I forget?" he replied, sounding just as fond of the memory as Marissa was. "The cool water was such a relief after a week of record highs. And it was so dark out there, we could even see a few stars."

How perfectly she remembered that day. He'd refused to tell her where they were going, and so she hadn't brought anything to swim in. At first, when she saw the pool, she'd balked, but then he, along with the heat, had persuaded her to throw caution to the wind and they'd both leapt into the pool in nothing but their underwear, laughing and splashing like children. And then, when he'd swum toward her to point out the twinkling sight of Venus peeking through the dim glow of the city, she'd wrapped her arms and legs around him and pretended she couldn't see it, just to keep him so close. In the end, the episode hadn't managed to actually cool them down at all. But it had been one of the best evenings of her life.

Khalid seemed to be recalling the same things, because his smile faded, and his expression grew more intense, as though his thoughts were far away. In that moment, Marissa felt like not a day had passed since their separation. Their connection was as strong as ever.

Then he shook his head, inhaling deeply. "We're lucky we got away with it. Think if the future prince of Rifaisa had been caught breaking and entering."

Marissa saw the wistful look in his eyes and let herself reach for his hand across the table, rest hers gently over it. "You must be burdened with so many responsibilities now," she said. "I can't imagine what it would be like. But it must be rewarding, too, to be trusted by so many people."

Khalid nodded, not moving his hand. "It is. Vastly. It is what I was born to do." Then he pulled his hand away and used it to lift a forkful of potatoes to his mouth.

For a few moments, they both turned to their plates. The food was spectacular, every bite perfectly seasoned and cooked, but Marissa soon stopped tasting it, lost in her thoughts of the man sitting across from her. In some ways he was so much like the Khalid she'd once loved—sometimes so quick to show his emotion, other times mysterious, but always one hundred percent focused on the person he was with. But in other ways he had changed—grown up a great deal in such a short time. Though he'd had big professional goals before, now he was helping to rule a wealthy nation in a tumultuous part of the world. The stakes were high, and stress would be his daily companion. And yet his only complaint was about the lack of privacy. The same old Khalid, yet somehow different. Stronger.

What had not changed even in the slightest was the chemistry between them. When they'd first met, it had sizzled like butter melting in a hot pan. As they'd fallen in love, it had only grown more fierce. And in bed, it had been as powerful as a lightning bolt. When they made love the first time, she'd wondered if she'd dreamed it, it had been so intense and surreal. And now, even after three years, she still woke in the middle of the night from dreams of him to find her sheets damp with sweat and the familiar moistness between her legs. What she wouldn't have given, in all this time, to have that passion back, even just for one night. And now, he was here, so close, just a dining table away from her, and though she knew she should be telling him everything she'd come here to tell him and then moving on with her life, she wanted much more than a conversation. Wanted *him*, even if only for one last time.

She forced herself to tamp down those thoughts and concentrate on chewing, swallowing, and ignoring the rush she felt every time she looked up from her plate and found his eyes fixed on hers. When she gave up on food and pushed her plate away, the old lighthearted Khalid surfaced once again. "Come," he said, dropping his fork to his plate with a clatter and tossing his napkin aside. "Let's have dessert on the balcony."

OUTSIDE, in the warm humid air of Cairo, Khalid felt some of the tension between them diffuse slightly and was vastly relieved. He'd been annoyed from the moment she'd arrived at his door to discover that instead of the bitterness and cold he usually felt when he thought of her, he was overcome with a desire he'd assumed was long dead. Leave it to Marissa Madden to show up to a "closure dinner" looking so goddamned beautiful. She'd always had a talent for dressing in conservative clothing and yet looking tantalizing at the same time. The first time he'd seen her she'd been in a suit jacket and trousers and looked sexier than most women did in lingerie. Tonight, in that fitted outfit of frilly blouse and abbreviated skirt, she seemed miles long and unbearably feminine. His first thought had been to put his fingers in that curly bun of hers and shake it down over her shoulders, so he could wrap her long, dark hair in his hands and see if it still smelled of vanilla and ginger the way he remembered.

Of course, he'd done no such thing. His intent was for *her* to be taken off guard, not him. So he'd forced a light smile and sat down to dinner with her, trying not to let her do the thing she'd always done, where with a few of her soft smiles and understanding comments he found himself telling her everything on his mind. He could sit stone-faced through massive financial dealings with leaders of state now. He could certainly get through a dinner with an ex-lover without spilling his guts.

But for one moment tonight, he wished he didn't have to keep it all inside. Wished that when she took his hand and spoke to him about the trust his people had in him, he could have told her how much he had trusted her, and how it had felt when she'd betrayed that trust.

No. He would never let her know how much she'd hurt him.

"One second," she said, heading back inside the suite. She returned with a candelabra that minutes earlier had been sitting, unused, on one of the various side tables inside his suite. "It's too dark out here," she said by way of explanation. "I have to see what I'm eating."

The air was dead still. He took the box of matches from her and lit the candles, one by one, and watched the light flicker across the balcony and over her face as she sat down at the small bistro table and angled her chair toward the view. "Do you know how amazing this is, Khalid?" she asked, her eyes filling with wonder. "To be dining with the pyramids in the background? I mean, you must see things like this all the time. But you don't take it for granted. Promise me."

Khalid took nothing for granted. No one who'd grown up in the foster-care system ever could. But then, he reminded himself, he almost had once with Marissa. He had been so sure of her love for him. And he'd been so surprised to discover how fickle her feelings had truly been.

"I know," Khalid said, ignoring his own train of thought and pushing down the irritation. "It's spectacular. And the sight from my balcony at home is just as amazing. It's my favorite place in the palace."

As if she could imagine it herself, she closed her eyes and sighed. Then her eyes popped open again playfully. "But do you have desserts like this at the palace?" she asked. "These figs are amazing." She spooned up a mouthful of the ruddy fruit and syrup and slipped it into her mouth like it was her last meal on earth. "Mmm."

Something about the sight of her taking that bite—so slow and sensual that he felt himself stir below—pushed Khalid's brimming annoyance over into full-blown irritation.

"I'm glad you're enjoying it," he said abruptly, setting his own spoon to the side with disinterest. "But the time has come for you to tell me what you needed to tell me so badly. When I saw you earlier today, you seemed so desperate to talk to me. Now you're sitting here on my balcony lighting candles and lingering over dessert like we're having a romantic date. Which we're not."

Marissa blinked, clearly surprised at his outburst. Even he knew it was somewhat uncalled for. But how could he possibly explain what he really wanted: her out of his suite before his anger toward her was completely overwhelmed by desire.

"I'm sorry," she said, also pushing her dessert bowl away. "You're right. And it's getting late. We both have big days ahead of us, no doubt."

At this Khalid only nodded, keeping his gruff demeanor as armor.

Marissa went on. "The thing is, you caught me by surprise earlier, when you told me your marriage had ended. I needed some time to gather my thoughts."

"And now?"

"And now I'm not sure they're any clearer than they were when you first broke the news," she said warily. "I came here to tell you, among other things, how badly I'd been hurt when I found out you were getting married. I know we had fallen out of communication for a few months—and there was a very good reason for that, I promise—but still the news came as a terrible blow to me back then."

Khalid tried not to scoff. He knew exactly what her "very good reason" was, and had no interest in discussing that humiliation further. "I'm sorry if you were surprised when I moved on," he barked coldly. "But I did what I had to do."

Marissa shook her head. "Please let me finish. I said that I meant to tell you how much I felt betrayed when you married. But now that I know everything about the situation—" She paused for a moment, searching his face for something, and he tried to keep it a mask of disinterest. "The thing is, I didn't know that what we had between us would still feel so *real*, even after all this time. It makes me wonder if, maybe, finding each other in Cairo was no accident. Maybe we were meant to be together tonight."

Khalid groaned at this, let his head tip back in his chair. Why did she have to make this so impossible for him? Any man could see she was beautiful, and sexy as hell. He wanted nothing more than to have her again. And then she sat there, her body just feet from his, babbling on about what was meant to be? As if she had never betrayed him, never broken all those promises?

He balled his hands into fists, uncertain what to do. He could send her away—that seemed surely the smartest move.

Or he could enjoy her body, one last time. Take her as his again, and with the act, chase out the demons of the past she seemed to bring with her. Even the way she was looking at him now, her eyes uncertain, her lips pressed together, he recognized the attraction and longing shimmering within. She would enjoy every moment of their passion. Almost as much as he would.

He cursed softly, under his breath. "Marissa," he said, his voice thick as he rose and moved to stand above her chair. "We can't be together again—not the way we were. Surely you understand. I have responsibilities you could never be a part of."

After all, he would need to be able to trust the woman he let into his life. He would never again trust this one. "But you can't sit there and look so incredibly tempting and tell me you feel it all coming back and expect me not to want you."

He moved a step back, and then took her by her hand and lifted her out of her seat, so that she stood mere inches from him. "And I do want you," he growled.

And then, his body took over, and he lowered his head and captured her lips in a fiery kiss.

AT FIRST, Marissa did nothing, afraid to move and risk ending the kiss, afraid to kiss back and risk acquiescing to something she knew wasn't right. Here was the man who had left her behind, and then, when she'd been at her lowest, married someone else.

Here was a man who could melt her from the inside out with just one kiss.

It was hopeless. She kissed him back, and let all reason slip away.

His lips were full and soft, just as she'd remembered them. His kiss was insistent, demanding, and it filled her with desire. She pressed back, then let him break away for a moment only to angle his head and kiss her even more deeply. She felt his hands grip her shoulders and yank her closer to him, and she realized her arms had been hanging limply by her sides all this time. It was as if she'd lost control of her body. Ceded it over to him.

Now, pressed to him and held there by his strong hands, she felt the memories of every kiss they'd ever shared mingle with the sensation of this one, making her dizzy. His mouth opened and hers with it, and he ran his tongue slowly along hers, a taunting action that promised so much more. Urging him on, she snaked her fingers up the silken weave of his sweater, and then, when that sensation wasn't enough, lowered them again to slip underneath the hem and press them against the bare skin on his back. It was like running her fingers over one of the pristine marble artifacts she'd seen in the museum—the muscles firm, the skin of his back perfectly smooth, and the sensation that she was doing something forbidden overwhelming. Intoxicating.

As he nibbled at her lips, teased her with his tongue, she let herself fall further into the fantasy she'd had so many nights, the fantasy that, just for this moment, was becoming real. Every inch of her front, from to tops of her legs up her pelvis and to her breasts, was pushed tightly against him, heated by his body, feeling the rise and fall of his breath as if it were her own. She felt his arousal grow and knew her own would be just as apparent if he were to slide one of his large, warm hands up her bare leg, underneath her skirt. The thought of that happening was too much, and she shuddered slightly. He stopped his kiss for a moment, locked eyes with her, and dipped back for her lips even more intensely than before. He had seen the need in her eyes, of that she had no doubt.

Now his hands were in her hair, tugging it down from the precarious twist it had been in, and she felt it tumble across her shoulders. He reached for it and pulled his lips from hers to cup a mass of hair in his hands and bring it to his nose, inhaling as deeply as if it were a bunch of flowers. The gesture was so incredibly intimate that it stopped her in her tracks.

"Wait," she said, pulling her body away from his with anguish. "What's happening?"

Khalid opened his hand and let her dark hair slide through his fingers. He ran his hand up the side of her cheek and cupped her chin. "*Habibti,*" he murmured softly, a word Marissa had never heard before. It sounded seductive, but then what wouldn't have in his throaty whisper? "It's been so long since I've had you in my arms. Stay here, just for tonight." He tilted her face up, forcing her to look into his heavy-lidded eyes and see the desire reflected back at her within them.

Marissa's throat went dry with need. "I should go," she tried to say, though the words came out in only a raspy whisper.

Khalid's brow wrinkled with a frown. "Is there someone else?" he asked, releasing her face, stepping back an inch.

Frantically she shook her head no. "No one," she admitted. *Not since you,* she thought, but thankfully managed not to say.

He grabbed her hand in his and held it to his chest. "Then stay. See how one kiss sends my heart pounding?" He stopped for a second and moved their hands to just above her left breast. "And yours too. We're here, together, just for tonight. Why shouldn't we let ourselves have something that you know as well as I do will be amazing? Who will we be hurting?"

A thought flashed into Marissa's mind: *me.* It would be her that could get hurt if she let this happen. "You don't know how long I wished to have this again," she said, her voice choking with emotion and longing. "But."

"But you are in Cairo," Khalid interrupted. "And I am too. Even you said you believed we were both here for a reason. What other reason could there possibly be?"

She sighed and closed her eyes for a moment, as if she hoped that ridding herself of the sight of Khalid would somehow erase the temptation. It was useless—she could still feel the heat on her cheek where his hand had been. She opened her eyes again and searched his face for an answer. "Only tonight?" she asked him at last, knowing that an evening of pleasure with Khalid would be worth any amount of pain later.

"Tonight, but there will be no *only* about it, I promise you that," he uttered, and again he bent his head and pressed his lips to hers in another dizzying kiss.

THIS TIME, when Khalid kissed Marissa, she kissed back. Passionately. Her lips parted for him and her tongue met his and licked playfully, then darted back and licked again. The sensation of her surrender—of knowing she was his, absolutely, if only for tonight—drove him wild. Not for the first time he recalled how unsatisfying other women had been in their three years of separation. She was so different—so complete in her desire, utterly absorbed in the act. In that respect, at least, she hadn't changed at all. When he pulled back for a breath, she leaned back and shook her head side to side, driving back the tumble of hair from her face, then stepped closer to him and ran her hands up his arms, leaving them energized somehow. He wound his own arms around her waist to pull her even closer, and leaned down to connect his lips once more with hers.

This close, her breasts seemed to press more insistently against him. He hated to ignore them, picturing their creamy roundness, but forced himself to linger longer on her lips, nibbling first the top lip and then the bottom, softly at first, and then with just the slightest scrape of his teeth. She moaned into his mouth and he pulled her in tighter still. Then he raked his lips from hers and dragged them over to the place just below her ear, where he kissed a trail behind to where her hair became soft wisps. With one hand still around her waist, he moved the other to push away the curls and graze her neck, then kissed the sensitive skin at the nape. With his tongue, he retraced his path, taking the lobe of her ear gently into his mouth and suckled. Sneaking a peek at her face he saw that her eyes were closed, her mouth parted in an inaudible gasp of pleasure. The sight made his burgeoning erection swell further, and in response, she wriggled her pelvis closer to him.

At that, it was he who was gasping. If there had been any question of her intentions before, there were none now, now that she pressed her warmth against him hungrily. She wanted him. But she would have to wait.

Still lapping at her ear, Khalid used his other hand to lift up her chin, giving him easy access to the long line of her neck. First he stroked it up and down with his fingers as slowly as he could muster, then he kissed where his hands had been, making a lazy path from her jaw to the collar of her shirt. Undaunted by her moans, he opened the collar and pushed the fabric aside, continuing down to her collarbone, where he nipped and licked the ridge and then—gently, incredibly gently—lapped his tongue in a tiny circle in the divot where the collarbones met. Her moans stopped suddenly, and he knew she was focusing intently on the sensation, so he lingered there a moment longer. And then, unable to delay himself for even one more second, he tore his lips from her flesh and set about the business of stripping her naked.

At the very first button, she seemed to regain consciousness, and she covered his hands with hers. "Let's go inside," she murmured. "Come with me." Still holding his hand, she turned and made her way through the balcony door, her hips swaying as she stepped into the cool quiet of his suite. The sight of her from behind threatened to be his undoing. As soon as they were both clear of the dining room table, he scooped her up and carried her down the stairs, through the living room, and back up to his bedroom. With her still balanced in his arms, he threw open the French doors but didn't bother to close them again—after all, tonight, no bodyguards would be stationed inside his quarters, no aides would barge in. Tonight, they would have the kind of privacy he'd forgotten could even exist. And he would make the most of it.

"Khalid," Marissa whispered, looking up into his eyes beseechingly. "I need you now. Don't make me beg."

He smiled at her words. Begging would be only the beginning. "I make no promises, Habibti," he rasped, laying her on the enormous four-poster bed. Still standing, he leaned above her and unbuttoned the white blouse she wore, one button at a time. As each new inch of flesh became exposed, he caressed it, running his fingers through the valley between her breasts, over the white lace of her bra, and then down her belly. She gasped and sucked in her stomach when he reached the area around her navel, but that only made him laugh. "Relax," he told her. "You're every bit as sexy as I remember." Then he sealed the statement with a string of kisses across her soft stomach.

Next he removed her shoes, lingering just as long on the curve of her instep and the angles of her anklebone, before making his way up her long, bare legs, up to the knee, where he abandoned her yet again, just to watch the expression of frustration cross her face. "Patience," he told her. "I intend to make this last."

With that he reached for the zipper on the side of her skirt and pulled it down. When she was free of the skirt, he finally allowed himself to take in the full sight of her, raking his eyes over her near-naked body. But she was not naked enough, he decided, sliding his fingers underneath her white bra, pressing the cups aside so he could take first one nipple, and then the next, between his fingers.

Groaning, Marissa reached behind her back to unclasp her bra, throwing it to the side. Then she went to work on him, reaching up to pull off his sweater. He allowed it, ducking his head as it slid over his shoulders. He knelt on the bed next to her so he could run his hands over her breasts and down, down to her panties.

The touch was more than she could take. She propped herself up on her elbows and then popped up to a sitting position, then pushed him down by the shoulders on his back. Before she could work the belt from his trousers, he rolled them both over, wriggling out of his pants all the while and kicking them to the side of the bed. "I said patience," he muttered, but already he knew it was too late, his need was too urgent. He had to be inside her and could not wait.

"Forget patience," she cried. "I need you, Khalid. Now." And with that she pulled off her white panties and grabbed his hand, putting it between her legs—where he found her hot, wet, and inviting. It was too much. He dragged his body away from her, to the top of the bed, where he knew he would find a box of condoms. He grabbed one and tore it from its packaging, then he returned to her where she lay flushed and wild-eyed. In a flash his boxers were gone, the condom was on, and he was atop her. And then, like his life depended on it, he slipped inside.

It was sweet, as amazing as he'd remembered, making love to her, pulling his hips back slowly and thrusting once more inside her warmth over and over again. The rhythm of it was so easy, so natural, and yet each push and pull made the dizzying rush behind his eyes mount, until he had to close them and think of anything—anything—other than the sight of her lifting her hips to him below, the way she arched her head back and seemed utterly unleashed. But even with his eyes closed, he felt the contraction and release of her muscles around his shaft as he filled her, and the sensation threatened to undo him. She reached up her hands, smacked them flat on his chest, forcing his eyes wide open and his desire up another degree. She pushed him so he'd lean back and angle his thrusts upward. And then when she'd arranged him exactly where she wanted him, she grabbed onto him and whispered, "There. Oh please, God, right there."

There was no question she was close. The tightness seemed to increase around him as her moans grew more frantic. She was gripping his biceps like her life depended on his every move. He shifted his balance ever so slightly to free up one hand, then reached around to her bottom and squeezed the muscled flesh there in the same rhythm of their sex, adding to the intensity of every inward push. Finally, when he knew she was at the edge, he leaned down to graze her nipple with his teeth. She screamed out his name, the first syllable distinguishable but the second only a frantic cry. The shuddering of her around him became more than he could bear, and he tumbled down after her into that bottomless well of pleasure.

When he was completely spent, he let himself surrender to the heaviness in his limbs and rolled to the side, lying on his back with a relaxed moan of satisfaction. Out of the corner of his eye, he saw her chest heaving up and down, her eyes closed and her face completely relaxed. For a long moment, he thought she might slide off into sleep—it certainly was a promising prospect for him, and he let the world grow a little dimmer in that perfect relaxation of contentment. But before he was fully out, he felt her soft hand on him again, curling around the base of his penis. He propped himself up on his elbows.

"My God, Marissa. Again, already? You'll kill me," he groaned playfully. But then he saw the look in her eyes wasn't playful at all. It was a look of shock.

"It's not that," she stammered, and at last he looked to where she was staring, where her hand held his most sensitive area. What he saw was not what he expected, and he gasped.

"The condom," he uttered.

Marissa nodded. "It broke."

4

For several seconds, the world around Marissa stopped turning.

From somewhere very far away, she saw Khalid raising himself off the bed, rushing to the en suite bathroom, where he was doubtlessly taking off the wretched condom. She heard him swearing, and the water in the sink running and then turning off. He would be coming back in here, she knew, and she knew too that now she had to tell him everything. She should have done it before. But at the last minute, when over dessert Khalid had demanded she tell him why she was there, she'd panicked and decided against telling him about the baby she'd lost. And then he'd surprised her with that kiss, and as much as she hated to admit it, she'd let herself go along for the ride, be swept away by the sensation of Khalid's lips and hands and body. All thoughts of confession had gone out the window along with her composure.

Until now. Now she had no choice but to face what had happened and what she'd kept from him for so long. And it terrified her.

The bathroom door opened with force and slammed against the doorstop, adding to her anxiety. Khalid, still naked and magnificent, stood with a look of annoyance in his eyes exactly like the one that had been there when he'd first spotted her at the hotel restaurant. Suddenly the bedroom, so hot and close a moment ago, felt icy cold. She shivered and pulled the plush white comforter up around her body as a shield.

"Are you on any other form of birth control?" he demanded.

Marissa shook her head. Taking a pill every day had seemed a pointless waste after she'd realized he was never coming back for her. And since then, there had been no one interesting enough to make her come out of her self-imposed celibacy.

Khalid only grunted. "Where are you in your cycle?"

She looked up at the ceiling, as if she would find a calendar there. Or maybe an escape hatch. "The middle," she told him after counting back the days in her head.

"If I remember correctly from Biology 101, that's the dangerous time," he said gruffly.

She nodded.

"Shit," he growled. His face was as hard as stone but his eyes spoke volumes. Anger. Irritation. *Regret.* "Shit, shit, shit."

Marissa nodded again. Then the tears started.

She tried to choke them back, but they came too fast. She tried to breathe deeply for calm but it was useless, just a sputtering, lip-trembling, inward gasp. Humiliated, she buried her face in the comforter, too embarrassed at her emotional response to even look at him.

"Oh, for the love—stop crying," he commanded, which only made her cry harder. "Oh, hell." He did nothing for a long time, and let her cry, and soon she felt the flow of tears provide their calming release. He seemed to sense this, or perhaps he heard her sniffles slow. "Marissa," he said, more softly. "Marissa, please." He sat down on the bed next to her and put an arm around the lump of covers she'd become. "Don't cry. This isn't your fault. No one could have predicted this would happen."

"That's just it," she murmured from underneath her tent of bedcovers. "It's happened before."

There was a long period of silence.

"What?" he said at last.

She repeated herself, not moving the protective duvet.

He yanked a corner of it up and leaned his head low so he could see her. "I heard what you said," he scolded. "But I want to know what it means."

With a sigh, she moved the duvet completely away from her face, knowing that her smeared eye makeup and tear-stained cheeks should be the least of her concerns now. "I had a pregnancy scare back when you were in America," she began. "Right at the time when your grandfather found you, actually."

"But you were on the pill then," Khalid said, his face an unreadable mask. "You had your period like clockwork."

"I was careless, and I forgot a pill," she explained. "And they say it's only 99 percent effective if you take it at the same time every day—no mistakes."

"You never mentioned any mistakes to me."

"That's because I was sure it was a false alarm. And then after a few more days, when my period still didn't come, I decided to buy a pregnancy test so we could find out the news together." The memory of that day slammed into her, and she felt her eyes well up again.

"Why didn't you, then?" Khalid's voice was growing impatient.

"I did. That was where I went that morning. The morning when you found out—who you were."

That stopped his questions dead. He leaned back a little, propping himself up on his hands, and looked off into the distance, as if he too were remembering every detail of that fateful morning. "I don't understand. You went out for bagels. You were so hungry you rushed out the door like a bat out of hell." He paused, processed this, and then groaned. "Of course you rushed.

Because you were off to the pharmacy for a home pregnancy test."

Marissa nodded, exhaled again on a long sigh. "But when I got home, there was no chance to talk to you. You were gone so fast there was no time to think."

Khalid turned to her and brushed one rogue tear off her face with the rough pad of his thumb, a sympathetic gesture that reminded her of all that they used to have. "I'm sorry, Marissa. I'm sorry I left you alone with that burden. I had no idea, but I should have taken the time to let you tell me. So you wouldn't have been left with that hanging over your head." His words were more comforting than the duvet around her shoulders, and for the first time since she'd seen the broken condom, she let herself look him in the eyes, to try to show him how grateful she was for his understanding.

But then he went on and shattered that illusion. "But it doesn't matter now, does it? Obviously, it was a false alarm then. And that's what this will be, too. The chances are one in a million."

She squeezed her eyes shut for a moment. Of course he'd assume it was a false alarm, since she'd never told him anything. And now, when she explained the truth, he would be furious. She steeled herself for his anger, wishing she could be anywhere but there, about to say what she had to say: "It wasn't a false alarm. I was pregnant."

As soon as the words were out of her mouth, Marissa straightened her shoulders, as if she had to be ready for a physical onslaught instead of just an emotional one. What would he say to her? What horrible accusations would he make? He'd be so busy ranting at her she'd never be able to make him listen, understand her side of the story. She inhaled, ready to plead her case, to beg him to forgive her and to try to understand what she'd been thinking.

But Khalid was silent. He did not rant, did not shout, did not leap off the bed and point his finger at her accusingly or throw the bedside lamp to the floor in fury. He said nothing at all. He didn't look at her either. He simply stood up from the bed—the bed where only minutes ago they had been lost together in the kind of pleasure Marissa had nearly forgotten could exist—and turned away from her. And strode out of the bedroom, closing the French doors behind him with a soft click.

THE MOMENT KHALID was out of that suffocating bedroom, he found he could barely stand. He rushed to the guest bathroom and pulled on a fluffy hotel robe, belting it tightly around his waist, as if the terry cloth would some how keep out the onslaught of emotion. It did no such thing. He crumpled onto the nearest sofa, his hands in tight fists, then rose again after a few moments, when he decided that he could stand, but not breathe. With a few long strides, he made his way to the balcony, the place where he'd first given in to his damnable urges and kissed her tonight. The farthest point in the suite from where she was now.

Even out there, with the city noise and warm air and the darkness surrounding him—the candles had burned out into waxy puddles on the dessert table—he felt utterly raw. Minutes ago he'd been so lost in her body, so empty-headed with desire, that nothing could have hurt him. And then his mind went back to the moments after their lovemaking, when his illusions had shattered.

The way she'd wept when she had seen the broken condom, all he'd wanted in the world was to stop her tears. It had always been that way with them. He couldn't stand the sound of her snuffling—it wounded him in a way no injury could—but he'd learned in the year they'd been together that he had to let her cry just a little, that it was something she needed to do to feel better. God knew why.

And this time had been no different. He'd heard her sniffles slow and tried to tell her it was okay so she'd calm down, even when he knew that it wasn't okay—that the mere possibility of her accidentally becoming pregnant with his child—his *heir*—had him reeling. And then, as if that weren't enough, she'd thrown him a curveball so unexpected, so utterly surprising, he'd found there were no words to respond.

Of course, he now realized, it was exactly the sort of thing he *should* have come to expect from Marissa Madden. After all, he'd been gobsmacked when he'd learned she'd taken up with another man while his side of the bed was still warm. Why would it be that much more shocking to discover that at that very time, she'd also been pregnant with his child?

The words were like knives in Khalid's brain. Pregnant. *With his child.* A child he'd never known had existed. And where was that baby now? He thought he knew her well enough to believe that she would never have terminated a pregnancy without speaking with the father first, but now? He couldn't be so sure. The thought of it made his gut churn. That would be a betrayal beyond any he could imagine. He couldn't believe even she was capable of leaving him out of such an important decision.

And if she'd carried the baby to term? Then somewhere in America his baby was alone right now, growing up without his or her father, all because of her deceit.

As painful as that option was, he prayed it was the case. If so, that would mean he had a chance to make things right, now, when the baby was still young. Unbidden, an image of a sweet-faced little child, just over two years old, appeared in his mind, with Khalid's tan skin and the bright green eyes of his mother. His heart seized. To think, if he hadn't run into Marissa here in Cairo, that child would have grown up believing he'd been abandoned by his father.

No child deserved that.

Furiously pacing the small balcony, Khalid stole a look inside the suite. There was no movement. Was she still lying on the bed naked, he wondered, and despite himself, his groin stirred. Damn his sex drive. Look where it had gotten him. He'd take care to keep her at arm's length from now on. In fact, he realized, the sooner his lawyers took over and sued for custody, the better. If he played his cards right, there was a chance he'd never have to be alone with her again.

At that very thought, he heard the creak of the balcony door, and knew his private rumination had come to an end.

"Khalid?" she said.

He remained turned away from her. He was too angry to speak. He felt like yelling and stomping and breaking the glass dessert bowls all over the tiled balcony floor. Instead, he froze.

"Khalid," she said again, her voice more insistent. "Please turn around. There's more to this story than you know."

At that, he wheeled around. "More to the story than that you lied to me and gave birth to a child—my child—without my ever knowing?"

She swallowed. He saw the muscles working in her throat, saw the twisting of her face, and knew he would not like what came next. Then she nodded. "I lost the baby, Khalid," she whispered. "In a car accident in the fourth month. That's why I never told you, why I broke contact all those years ago. I was overcome with grief."

I lost the baby. With her words, all emotion drained from Khalid's body like water running into a drain. All the anger and fury were gone, but so too was that glimmer, however irrational, of hope and excitement at the prospect of becoming a father. So the accident he had read about had cost them their child. No wonder she'd stopped returning his calls and emails. No wonder she'd let her charade fall to the wayside. His shoulders sank, like he was bearing some great weight, and he heaved a sigh. He knew, but did not like, what he had to do next.

"Pack your bags," he told her. "Your vacation in Cairo is over."

He strode past her and moved into the suite with certainty, where he picked up his cell phone and started punching in numbers.

"What do you mean it's over?" Marissa called, rushing up to him, a frantic edge in her voice. "Who are you calling?" She put her hand on his to still the dialing. He stopped and fixed an angry gaze on her.

"I'm calling my assistant to tell him to make arrangements for a second traveler on my return to Rifaisa tomorrow," he said simply. "He'll need the night to arrange your visa, and see to the necessary additions in security."

"My visa? But I have a visa," she cried. "For Egypt. Where I'm staying for two more days, before going back to Las Vegas."

"I'm afraid not," Khalid said, crossing his arms in front of him. "That was what you *were* doing, before tonight. Now there is a change of plans. You're coming to Rifaisa with me, where you'll stay until I know whether you're going to be the mother of my child."

"That's preposterous." She crossed her arms in a mirror of his body language, as if her feminine frame could somehow stand up to his iron determination. "I'm going home. If I'm pregnant, believe me, you'll be the first to know."

Khalid scowled. "Just as I was the first to know about the child of mine you carried before?"

She gasped and reeled back as though he'd hit her. "I wanted —" she sputtered. "I wanted to tell you in person. I wanted to see the reaction on your face when I told you."

"Well, then, enjoy. You're looking at it right now."

Her lower lip started to shake, and he steeled himself for another bout of tears. This time she could cry herself dry, for all he cared. His heart felt like a brick in his chest. His throat felt tight.

"I'm not coming with you," she stammered. "I want to be with my family."

"Perhaps you don't understand," Khalid said, keeping his voice steady and cold. "There's a chance you're carrying the heir to the crown of Rifaisa. The future of my country. That is not something I take lightly. And since you can't be trusted for a second, even with something so sacred as this, you are coming with me. Am I clear?"

"You can't do this!"

"Look around you, Marissa. You're on my turf now. I can do whatever I choose. And I choose to keep you under my thumb, until we know for sure that you aren't pregnant."

"And if I am?"

"Then you'll become my wife," he said, iron running through his voice and ice through his veins. "In name only."

5

THERE WAS NO POINT IN ARGUING FURTHER. KHALID WAS IMMOVABLE. She finally persuaded him to let her stay through the end of her conference, though he claimed to agree only because he wanted to keep their situation from becoming public and not as a concession to her needs. Any thought of what she needed had gone right out the window when she'd told him about her miscarriage, and he'd showed her he was completely incapable of sympathy.

When had he become so heartless, she wondered? It wasn't as if he had ever been Mr. Sympathetic Male of the Year, but at least he'd tried, once upon a time, to be there for her in times of trouble. Now, after she'd told him about the greatest heartbreak of her entire life, he'd accused her of being untrustworthy and then made her a prisoner.

Back in her own hotel room, she thought of the Rifaisi security guard standing outside her door and felt like screaming. She would scream, if she didn't think that would have him breaking down the door to investigate in an instant. It infuriated her the way the guard had been so kind and solicitous to her, until she'd asked him about leaving the room and he'd replied with a monosyllabic grunt that she translated to "Absolutely not." As nice as he seemed, he took his orders from Khalid. It seemed everyone on this side of the world did.

And now, unless she wanted to cause an international incident, she did too. She paced through the spacious room, cursing herself and her idiotic notions about "closure." If this was closure, then she would prefer to leave things wide open, thank you very much. How Grant would laugh when she told him how right he'd been. Except he wouldn't laugh at all, because this was way past the point of being funny, she thought with a sigh.

And the worst part was, even as she railed against his dictatorial edict, she could see exactly where Khalid was coming from. She *should* have told him sooner about her pregnancy and the accident. Because of that mistake, she could understand why he wouldn't trust her this time around, why no amount of her promises would assure him. If only she had told him about the baby. If only he could understand why she hadn't.

She hardly slept at all that night, and when she did, her dreams were so dark she wished she'd stayed awake. The next day moved like molasses as her brain lived and relived the events of the night before. She managed to get through her meetings as though nothing were wrong—a skill she'd picked up when her brother had forced her out of bed three months after the car accident and insisted she throw herself into her work. At the time, she'd resisted, but as the weeks had passed, she'd found her gift for the work made up for her lack of motivation. Campaign after campaign had come off with great success, and slowly, the grief of her loss had faded. It had never disappeared. But it had eased up quite a bit, and with it, the dream of a second chance with Khalid.

Well, now she had her second chance. But this was not how she'd imagined it. Not at all.

She was weary from forcing herself through her day when she got back to her hotel room that night. Her new bodyguard trailed behind her and stopped right outside the door. Marissa decided it was a good evening for room service and a hot bath. After all, this might be her last chance at privacy for a long time. Come tomorrow, she'd be traveling to Rifaisa for the first time, along with Khalid and his squadron of aides. And then she'd be trapped there for two weeks. Maybe more.

Maybe forever.

Pushing the thought away along with her high heels, she changed out of her constricting suit jacket and pants and slipped into the sheer cotton drawstring pants and matching tank she'd brought as pajamas. She retrieved the room service menu and flopped onto her plush bed, turning on the TV absentmindedly as she flipped through the list of offerings. Nothing appealed to her until she got to the desserts. There she saw a list of familiar treats: cheesecake, apple pie, molten chocolate cake, and some flavors more native to Egypt. She was seized by the urge to order three desserts and call it a night, and was about to pick up the phone and do just that when her eye caught a description of a dish of figs, almonds, honey, and cinnamon, soaked in rich syrup—the dessert she'd had on her lips when Khalid had kissed her last night. She dropped the menu and sighed deeply, lost in the memory of his touch.

Despite herself, despite the horrible situation it had landed her in, she did not regret one second of their lovemaking. Yes, she wished she'd never run into him, wished she hadn't gone to his suite, wished like hell that condom hadn't broken, but she couldn't wish away the passion they'd shared. That was something too rare, too sacred, and too powerful to ever regret.

Her appetite vanished and she gave up on dinner. Instead she drew herself a bath in the expansive tub, filled it with rose-scented salts, and surrounded her body with the warm water. A poor substitute for Khalid's arms, but a much safer one. She closed her eyes and sank deeper into the suds. Her problems started to retreat from her mind. She sighed deeply, imagining herself on a beautiful white boat, sailing across the ocean and away from her troubles. She could almost hear the seagulls in the distance and smell the salt in the air.

Then she heard the unmistakable sound of a key card beeping at her door.

Still in the bathtub, she froze. Who was at her door? What had happened to Khalid's guard? How could anyone have gotten a key? She listened hard and heard the unmistakable sound of the latch releasing and then the door opening and closing with a hushed click. She should scream, she thought, but nothing came out of her mouth. And then it did—a high-pitched, piercing squeal that impressed even her. She followed it up with a loud "Help!" and then launched her dripping body out of the tub and toward the heaping pile of folded towels nearby. "Help!" she hollered again.

The bathroom door flew open noisily, and Marissa frantically pulled a white towel to her breasts. "Get out!" she cried, looking for a weapon, but before she'd managed to grab hold of the nearest heavy object—a thick glass soap dish—she'd identified her intruder. Her jaw dropped open and she dropped her towel in shock.

"What are you doing here?" she demanded, reaching down as modestly as possible to grab the towel back up and wrap it around her body tightly. Just three feet away from her shivering naked form, Khalid stood at the bathroom door with a wicked smile on his face, arms crossed in front of him like he were watching a show. Annoyance at the fright he'd given her mingled with a tingle of awareness, as he looked her up and down, taking her in as though the towel were as transparent as cellophane. It was true what they said, she thought. The sensations of alarm and sexual attraction were easily confused.

"Enjoying your bath?" he asked. His eyebrow was quirked in a way that told her that he was enjoying the *thought* of her bath. Very much.

"I was," Marissa spat, pushing down the sexual jolt his scrutiny brought with it. "Until you *broke into my hotel room*."

"I knocked for what felt like a lifetime," he told her. "Then I started to worry. After a few minutes, my head of security spoke to the hotel management and explained that you were under my protection. They produced a key card in no time flat." He gave her a nonchalant shrug, as if it were everyday state business to break into a woman's private room while she tried to relax inside. "I should have known you were in the bath all along. You always tried to hide in the tub whenever you wanted to avoid the world."

Marissa groped for the hotel bathrobe, sparks of anger flashing behind her eyes. "Is it any wonder I'm trying to hide when I'm about to be kidnapped?"

Khalid sighed, and the smile on his face subsided somewhat. "You're being a tad dramatic, Marissa. I'm treating you to a luxurious trip to one of the most prosperous nations in this part of the world. Everything will be first-class—you'll want for nothing. And odds are good it'll only be a couple of weeks. Then you can put Rifaisa—and me—as far behind you as you'd like. Finally have the *closure* you were so intent on."

He uttered this last bit with such spite Marissa winced. "This," she told him, "is not the closure I had in mind. I still don't understand why you won't let me go back to Las Vegas. You're a powerful man. Surely you can have me followed around like a criminal there just as easily as you can here."

He shrugged. "Probably. But I've always said, when you want something done right, do it yourself." Then, with a more serious tone, he added, "Besides, staying close to me is in your best interests, too. There are people out there who would find you a valuable kidnapping prospect if they knew what was going on. And I don't want you to find out what a real kidnapping feels like. Suffice it to say it wouldn't involve any long, hot soaks in the tub."

She shuddered, not from the chill of the room after the warm bath, but at the truth of what he said. He was a powerful, wealthy man involved closely in the oil business. That made him a target. And targets had a way of radiating out from their centers.

"I don't mean to scare you, Marissa," he said, reaching over and draping the bathrobe she'd been clutching over her shoulders. "Just to impart to you the seriousness of the situation." His hands lingered on her arms as he wrapped the robe around her. Despite her common sense, Marissa took comfort in them for a moment. Then she turned her back to him so she could shimmy free of the towel underneath and belt the robe tightly around her waist.

"Have you told anyone about this?" he asked to her back.

Marissa paused, glad her face was hidden from him. "Just Knox," she said. "I had to explain why I wasn't coming back right away." She didn't add that she'd also called Grant and Jenna and told them she'd be extending the trip. They were as good as family, and she trusted them with her life, but Khalid might not see it that way. She turned back around, and forced a smile at him. "Tell me you at least trust Knox." Knox, after all, had introduced them in the first place, and he'd always treated Khalid like a member of the large, rowdy Madden clan.

Khalid looked up for a moment. "As much as I trust anyone, I suppose," he said at last, and his words angered her. She pushed past him through the bathroom door and into the main living area.

"More than you trust me." She headed for her clothes draped on the bed.

Khalid followed her and whirled her around, a dark look in his eyes. "You think I don't wish things were different?" he growled. "I'm just as trapped in this situation as you are."

The words stung bitterly. She hated that he felt trapped by her. Hated the scorn that was written all over his face. "Then let me go." She twisted out of his grasp. "I have a loving family waiting for me back in Las Vegas. With their help, I can take care of myself, and a baby too, if I need to. I don't need you."

Her words only incited him further. "Is that what you want? To raise a baby by yourself, a world away from his father?" His voice was low and bitter, barely more than a whisper. "To bring him or her up far from their birthright? Would you have your son wonder who he really was until he was my age, and only then watch him have to walk away from everything he knows—everything he loves—so that he can fulfill his duties as my heir?"

His pained words took the wind out of Marissa's sails. Khalid was talking about himself, of course, not some possibly nonexistent son. She'd never thought of what he'd gone through in quite that way. She'd always assumed he'd been glad to find out his true origins. Proud to take his proper place in Rifaisa. She'd never truly considered just how much he'd given up to do so.

She bit back all the anger that had been coursing through her and forced herself to imagine what that would have been like if it had happened to her. How she'd miss her family and friends and everything familiar. How lost she'd feel in such a strange country, where she didn't even speak the language.

Well, she was about to get a crash course in empathy, she thought. And if she was indeed pregnant, she would have to learn how to survive all that change permanently, just as Khalid had. For she knew as sure as she knew she was alive, he would not let his own child go through what he'd been through. And she would not want him to. If there was a baby, that baby would stay in Rifaisa. And that meant she would stay, too.

With a sigh, she let her shoulders go slack, her expression soften. She plopped down on the big bed and folded her hands in her lap. "If there is a baby," she said, all the anger out of her tone, "I want him to know who he is. But this whole discussion is most likely moot."

Khalid, too, relaxed his stance, and for a moment, she felt as though they could be partners in this mess. That they could handle whatever came their way together. Then he spoke, and the fantasy shattered. "Hopefully. In which case, believe me, I will be happy to return you to your family at the earliest opportunity."

The blast of reality reminded her who she was to him. Not a partner, and certainly not a lover. Only an annoyance, pure and simple. One that would be dispatched with as soon as possible. She tried quickly to cover up the hurt that realization caused. "I can hardly wait to book the flight," she said, hearing the pettiness in her voice.

"Soon enough," he replied. "In the meantime, I came here tonight to tell you the travel schedule and give you time to prepare. We fly to Dubai tomorrow at two, where my yacht is docked—"

"Your yacht?" Marissa interrupted, incredulous.

"Of course. I am the sheikh of an exclave whose livelihood depends on the ports that host every passing oil tanker coming from the north. We take our connection to the Gulf very seriously."

"But wouldn't it be faster to fly all the way—or drive?"

"Maybe. But it wouldn't be as beautiful. I'm allowed very little freedom in this life," Khalid explained, "and I like to spend it on the water."

Surprised, Marissa said nothing.

"Assuming mild seas, we'll be in Rifaisa before the night is out. That should allow us a low-profile entry to the palace."

She nodded. "Is there anything special I need to wear? Or do?"

Khalid frowned, then seemed to comprehend what she was asking and shook his head. "Rifaisa is a progressive area. Assuming you packed appropriately for Cairo, you'll be fine. Haven't you met Jana?"

"Yes, but." She trailed off, realizing just how ignorant she was of the place she was about to experience. "Of course. I'll follow her lead."

"She's an excellent role model," he said, and even that tidbit of praise raised an irrational flare of jealously in Marissa. She refused to acknowledge it. He folded his arms in front of his chest. "If you have any questions about protocol, speak to her."

In other words, Marissa thought, *don't bother me with petty details.* "I'll do that."

"Where's your phone?" Khalid's eyes darted around the room. "I'll program her mobile number into it so you can reach her at any time." She spotted it on the bedside table and unlocked it so he could input the information. She tried not to notice the fact that he had Jana's number memorized. Why should she care?

"There. If you need anything, call her." He dropped her phone on the bed where it bounced once, then he looked at her. "Before I go, I have to ask. Why would you throw away what we had for a tumble with Knox's B-school buddy? You might have hidden a mercenary side from me, but only a fool would take a few shiny baubles over an entire kingdom."

It FELT cathartic to finally say the words he'd kept inside since he'd first seen her in the restaurant. But they weren't getting the reaction he'd expected. She didn't look horrified or guilty. She looked utterly confused. "In your phone," he attempted to supply. "You just called Grant. That's Grant Blakely, right?"

"That's right."

"So you two are still together?"

"What?" said Marissa. "We're not together. We have never been together. For one thing, his wife Jenna—one of my best friends—would kill me. Wait, you didn't think—No."

"I didn't think. I knew. I got the entire case file. That car accident. I was out of my mind with worry until I learned you had been off diamond shopping with Grant Blakely, the biggest playboy in Vegas."

Marissa looked at him with complete blankness. Like she was

too angry to even scream. "Khalid, you're an idiot. How long have you been laboring under this misunderstanding? Months? Years? This entire time?"

Khalid found himself off balance. "I saw the headlines. I saw the photos."

"You believed a tabloid headline over me? You couldn't call me and ask? I was in the hospital. I had just lost my baby—your baby. You couldn't pick up the phone?"

Khalid stammered. "I don't have to explain myself to you." Didn't he, though? Could he have gotten it so wrong? He looked around, flailing for his footing in this shifting conversation. "You didn't cheat," he said at last.

"Of course I didn't."

"But you also didn't tell me about the baby. You kept my son or daughter from me."

"It was a complicated situation. There was a lot of grief. I thought I was saving you—"

"You thought you were saving an orphan from knowing about his own child?" he interrupted.

Marissa froze. Khalid felt the upper hand for a moment. "You see why it's so hard to trust you, don't you?"

Her mouth clamped shut.

"What you did," his voice trailed off while he tried to process the loss and betrayal.

"I know it is hard to trust me, Khalid, because of that, because of how you grew up, because of the whole picture. I get it. That's why I'm agreeing to go with you, and not calling the embassy and screaming bloody murder. But what you suspected of me and Grant, it's beneath you. I used to think it was beneath us." Marissa took a deep breath. "So I'll go with you. But I won't pretend to think you're the man I thought you were. That man would never have treated me this way."

6

THE NEXT DAY AT TWELVE-FIFTEEN, KHALID PACED THROUGH THE lobby of the Cairo Four Seasons trying to disguise his mounting annoyance to anyone who might be watching. Marissa was late, and lateness was unlike her. She'd always been obsessive about time, telling anyone who'd listen that her mother had taught her that punctuality was the greatest sign of respect. Now she was making him wait. He figured that showed exactly how much respect she had for him. Or maybe how much respect he'd lost last night.

He knew he shouldn't be surprised. Everything he thought he had known about the end of their relationship had been dead wrong. But she'd been keeping secrets, painful secrets, all the same. And between his misperceptions and her betrayal, they'd managed to lose everything.

Just thinking of it made his brain ache. With anger, yes, and fury at being lied to. But with heartbreak, too. Before, he'd only thought that accident had signified his loss of Marissa. Now he knew it was the loss of what could have been. A son or daughter. A child of their own.

He took a deep breath in and out, trying once more to contain his emotions. The last thing he needed was a hotel full of the world's most well-heeled travelers talking about how the Sheikh of Rifaisa looked upset or tired or whatever else they might imagine. And his own staff, who waited with him, needed to know his feelings even less. He shook off the loss, the strange displaced sense of grief, and looked again at his watch. Where was she?

And *who* was she? Marissa hadn't always been a devious person. He knew that in his bones. When they'd been together before, he couldn't think of a single time she'd seemed untruthful. In fact, sometimes she'd been too honest, blurting out far information than needed. He remembered one day, early in their relationship, when the waitress at a diner had asked her if she was having a good day. She'd answered that she was, except that her elderly cat Peter had just peed all over her only clean pair of jeans and as a result she was wearing a stinky pair from her dirty laundry. He laughed to himself now, remembering the waitress's polite "Ah" as she quickly backed away from their table.

As if conjured by his thoughts, Marissa stepped out of the elevator, looking just as sweet as the ripe berries he'd had on his cereal that morning. Her hair was pulled back into a neat, low ponytail. She wore a flowing pair of grey linen pants and a cropped violet V-neck sweater that outlined the shape of her breasts, and beneath it a cream-colored shirt narrowed to her waist. He was disappointed to see she'd chosen such a loose pair of trousers—it would make it harder for him to admire her abundant backside or the long legs that he'd so enjoyed having wrapped around him.

Then he scolded himself, remembering that she was not about to accompany him to Rifaisa as some kind of sexual plaything. Though if she were, she would be damned good at it.

"Good afternoon." She crossed the lobby and stopped feet away from him. "Thank you for sending for my baggage. I'm ready when you are." Her voice was cold. Good. It would make it easier for him to keep his distance.

"I was ready twenty minutes ago," Khalid snapped. "Come, the driver is waiting out front." He led her toward the big glass entryway, noticing the slow way she followed and the long looks she took at the amazing views on either side of them. "What kept you?" he demanded.

"I had an email to send," she said.

Khalid raised an eyebrow and held a door open for her to sail through. She'd made him wait for an email? Let the games begin.

"It was to my mom," she went on when they were outside in the hot Egyptian afternoon. "You know how if you say anything a little off to her, she'll get suspicious. I wouldn't want her sending Seal Team Six after me."

Khalid nodded. "So you decided not to tell her what was going on?" He spotted his driver in the circle, and gestured her over to the car.

Marissa nodded and followed. "Knox and I decided," she said. "She's on her first vacation in years. The first one since she left Dad."

When she said that, he snapped his head back to her quickly. "She left your father?"

She nodded again. "Last year. Don't pretend that you care, Khalid."

But he did care. As he ushered her into his car and slid in beside her, Khalid recalled the stories Marissa had told him about her father. How he'd cheated on her mother for years, expecting her to accept the betrayal as part of the cost of marriage. And she had, trying to keep her misery and her husband's philandering a secret from her children. She had, of course, failed miserably. Children, he knew all too well, had a way of sensing chaos around them. They got used to it, but they never forgot it was there. He certainly hadn't when he'd been bounced around foster homes, no matter how kind his caretakers were. He'd never forgotten that he would be moved, eventually, and there'd been no point in getting comfortable.

Inside the car, Marissa stared silently out the window at downtown Cairo speeding by, while Khalid was lost in thoughts of the past, recalling every time she'd confided in him about her parents' dysfunctional relationship. At the time, he had been sympathetic to her mother's distress, but deep down he'd felt Mrs. Madden was doing the right thing to keep the family together at all costs.

"Your mother," he said, startling her gaze away from the window. "She was brave to leave him, after all that time."

Marissa smiled at him, a beautiful, lit-up smile that tugged at his heart as it had always done, even though the smile wasn't meant for him. "Brave is exactly the right word," she said. "She always made excuses to stay. But when Natalie got the job in Chicago, there was no more pretending it was something she had to do for the children. We were all grown," she said, "and we wanted her to have her chance to be happy."

Natalie was Marissa's younger cousin whose parents had died when she was young. Marissa's parents had taken her in without question, despite having a many children of their own. One of the things Khalid had loved about Marissa was her big, open family. Her mother had been loving and generous, and her siblings had been accepting of him, despite the color of his skin or the troubles of his childhood.

"And is your mother happy?" he asked. "Now that she's rid of her heartless, cheating husband?"

"Don't forget that heartless cheater is my dad," Marissa said quickly. "But yes, she seems very happy. And I don't want to take away from her happiness with this nonsense with you, not unless this nonsense turns out to be more than a false alarm."

Khalid nodded. "All the more reason to keep this out of the papers," he said.

Khalid realized that he could never do to his own wife what

Marissa's father had done. Now, as a single man, he preferred to stick with women who knew what they wanted, and only wanted one night. It was easy. Uncomplicated. After going through a divorce in an Arabic nation, he had no interest in complications, not yet.

But here he was in the back of his limousine with Marissa Madden, who might be carrying his child. Who had once been pregnant with his child and never told him. Had she been with him back then, safe in Rifaisa, she never would have been in that car accident and never would have lost the baby. The very thought filled him with both grief and anger. He resolved to stop this back-and-forth, this friendly chatter. He didn't need to hear about her family, or anything else that could be considered even slightly intimate. He needed to keep her at arm's length.

With that, he reached down and grabbed his briefcase. Inside was his laptop, with plenty of distracting emails and paperwork that he needed to review. He booted it up, behaving as though she were no longer in the car. They rode the rest of the way to the airport in silence.

7

Marissa wasn't raised to go without by any stretch of the imagination, but she'd certainly never been on a private jet before. The flight to Dubai was a memorable experience, and one that she would have enjoyed a lot more under different circumstances—circumstances that didn't involve her suspicious, angry, unreasonable ex-boyfriend. She didn't know what she'd said, but after she'd told Khalid about her mother's divorce, he clammed up like a prisoner of war. He hadn't spoken another meaningful word to her the whole trip. They'd managed to navigate the private airport, make their way to the plane, and settle into seats just feet from each other without ever saying much more than "Here?" or "This way" to each other. After ten minutes of the uncomfortable silence that followed their boarding, Jana and the other aides had arrived and filled the remainder of the seats, chatting companionably, if totally incomprehensibly, with one another. Jana sat next to Marissa, probably instructed to do so by Khalid, and exchanged pleasantries in her lyrical English. From the looks of it, Jana had made trips like these time and time again. She seemed utterly comfortable despite a bumpy takeoff, and when tea was served, she turned to Marissa and said conspiratorially, "Ask for the almond cookies. They're amazing."

Marissa wished for a moment she could climb in Jana's head and borrow all the experience she had, so she wouldn't feel so totally on edge about everything that lay ahead of her. Since that wasn't an option, she asked Jana about her homeland instead.

The hour-long flight passed quickly after that. Jana's eyes lit up when she spoke about her tiny coastal exclave. She described the red-tinted sands east of the capital city, which were stained with iron oxide. Rust, Marissa realized with surprise. Jana nodded, and then explained that the beaches were pure white, the color of the coral that had created them. "After the beach, it is all desert sand, in every direction," Jana said of Rifaisa, "but every desert is different."

A fitting homeland for a man who seemed so hard and foreboding on the outside, Marissa thought. She stole a glance at him across the aisle of the jet. His mouth was set in a hard line, his eyes focused like lasers on the laptop open in front of him, his fingers dancing across the keys at lightning speed. What was it about that man that she found so fascinating? If he were a desert, she wanted to turn over every bit of sand within.

No, she realized. If he were a desert, he was the kind full of deadly snakes and scorpions. She needed to steer as clear as she could under the circumstances. Khalid had broken her heart over a stupid misunderstanding and left her to suffer the worst pain of her life alone. He could easily do it again.

By the time the group deplaned, Marissa had a much better idea of what to expect in Rifaisa, and a much better resolve to avoid the man who would one day rule it. And he seemed willing to let her avoid him, choosing to ride alone in his private car for the trip to the marina, leaving Marissa to go with the others. Relieved, she began to relax on the long drive, letting herself enjoy the sights of skyscrapers and exotic gardens that whizzed by her window. By the time they reached the dock and she laid eyes on the magnificent white yacht, the *Rifaisi Princess*—*how ironic* —bobbing gently in the bright blue-green waters, she had even let herself become a little excited at her upcoming adventure.

That excitement didn't last long. Rough seas from a windstorm coming in near their destination meant they would not be traveling on their intended schedule. They would stay here in the port until they had an all-clear from Rifaisa.

Jana translated the captain's announcement for Marissa as they boarded the craft, and then, seeing the American's worried expression, Jana smiled warmly and tried to reassure her. The yacht had very spacious chambers, she told Marissa. Spending the night aboard, if required, would be just as comfortable as a night in the palace.

But what Jana did not understand and Marissa could not explain was that there was something so isolated—so intimate— about being trapped on a vessel with Khalid, with no escape, even with the three aides and four bodyguards watching their every move. After all, hadn't Khalid proven on her first night in Cairo that he had a way of getting whatever privacy he desired? Could she protect her heart from him if they were alone together now?

She turned away from the others and leaned over the balcony of the yacht, staring vacantly out at the beautiful Persian Gulf. Again she reminded herself that Khalid was the last man on earth interested in being alone with her right now. He hated her for keeping the pregnancy from him. He hadn't spoken more than a grunt to her in three hours, and when he looked at her, which she'd seen him doing often, it was with narrowed eyes and a disapproving expression. She had nothing at all to worry about in that department.

Unfortunately, whispered some tiny voice in her unconscious. The voice remembered how amazing their lovemaking had been, despite its drastic consequences. She was fighting hard to ignore it.

"Would you like to see your room?"

Marissa started at the masculine voice, spinning around. While she'd been warring with herself, she had hardly noticed that the deck had cleared but for the very man she was going round and round about. Now he stood, hands on hips, just feet away from her. Alone. In the bright sun, he looked more tempting than the rows of comfy chaises that overlooked the sapphire sea below. Wouldn't she like to stretch out atop him...

Her ridiculous thoughts must have shown on her face, for he smiled just a little and raised his eyebrows sardonically. Like a panther he stalked closer, crowding the space between them and making his masculinity almost palpable. Clearly, he still enjoyed having the upper hand—though when he'd done it three years ago, it had seemed so much more playful and far less dangerous. "After all," he said in a low growl, "we could be stuck here for some time. You might want to rest. Or maybe take a bath?"

She forced all lascivious thoughts as far from her brain as she could and smiled serenely up into his face. "Actually, I'd love a bath. Maybe you have something I could read while I bathe? The National Examiner, perhaps? I hear it's very reliable."

He frowned at her jab.

She rolled her eyes. "Food would be great."

He nodded. "Follow me."

She followed him down into the belly of the ship, through a long twisting corridor that emptied, eventually, into a small stainless steel galley. Every surface shone silver or black, every inch of space packed efficiently with small versions of top-of-the-line appliances, knives, and pans.

"I've never seen such a masculine kitchen before," she said, working her eyes around the room, looking for just one soft spot or personal item and coming up empty.

"Thank you, I think," he said gruffly. "Have a seat." He held out a mahogany stool that had been nestled under a high counter and offered it to her, then took off his suit jacket and draped it over a wall hook.

"Are you cooking for me?" she asked, incredulous.

"Don't get too excited. My cooking is a regular occurrence these days."

She thought back to the times they'd cooked together in Las Vegas. He'd been a willing helper, and good with a chef's knife. But when it came time to apply heat to the food, he was a notorious scalder. "When did you learn to cook?"

"When I found out that I could get some privacy in the kitchen."

"You don't have a chef?"

He shrugged. Was it a stupid assumption, she suddenly wondered, to think that a prince would have his own personal chef to serve him at any beck or call? "I do. But he's understanding about letting me busy myself in the kitchen, and what can my staff say? I have to eat."

She smiled. "Very crafty of you, Khalid." His back was to her as he rustled in the fridge, and when he stepped out from behind the door, he held eggs, bundles of bright green herbs, and a round of goat cheese.

"Omelette?" he asked her.

"Yes, please," she answered. He turned back to the counter and set to work, leaving Marissa to watch and remember another time they'd made omelettes together: after the first time they'd made love. She'd insisted on taking things slowly, though it had killed her, and when finally she'd dropped her guard and let her passion go where it wanted to, it was nearly impossible to stop. They'd stayed awake half the night pleasing each other. When they awoke the next morning, they'd been ravaged with hunger. She had padded off to the kitchen wrapped in a towel, but no sooner had she poured the eggs into the pan, he'd arrived after her, slipping his arms around her while she tried to cook. He'd grabbed an edge of the towel and spun her toward him. She'd had to throw away that skillet—the eggs had been burned on permanently. But, oh, was it ever worth it.

Now look at him. He wasn't sitting there mooning over times past. He was whisking the eggs like a pro, chopping herbs and crumbling cheese like he'd done it all his life. If she were pregnant, would he cook for her just for fun, maybe make her whatever she craved, even in the middle of the night? More likely he would push her off on his chef, delegate her like another duty to be faced, another responsibility. How would she survive like that, ignored every day by a man she couldn't seem to get over, despite his past idiocy?

Or could he learn how to be part of a real family, when a family was thrust upon him?

"There's something I always wanted to ask you, after you left," she blurted, before she could think about what she was about to say.

"Oh?" He didn't take his eyes off the heating omelette pan.

"What was it like—suddenly having a family where you'd had none before? It seems like a pretty amazing sensation."

His face quirked. Was he, too, thinking of the family she might be growing inside her at this very moment? Then he took a deep breath and went back to his work. "It wasn't as amazing as you might think. Finding my grandfather—well, him finding me—that was wonderful. But when I got here I found that my more recent family legacy was as iffy as the one I'd had growing up in foster care."

Marissa rolled her lips together thoughtfully, wondering if she'd accidentally strayed into some sticky territory. "How so?"

Khalid inhaled deeply, as if preparing himself. "Growing up in foster care, I'd always known I didn't belong anywhere. For some reason, my parents hadn't wanted me, and the thought of that was painful. But I could imagine whatever I chose about their reasons for keeping me. That they were young, or they were poor, or even that they were dead."

Marissa gasped in a little.

"I know, it's crazy to think that I actually fantasized about dead parents. But then, that would have meant that they *did* want me. It was something, however small, to hold on to when I was a boy.

"Then I found out the truth, and it was nothing as romantic as I'd imagined. My mother was a one-night stand. My father was a selfish prince who didn't want to face what he'd done. He paid her off, and she dumped me off. Their lives went on as usual. Discovering all of that was hardly what I'd hoped for when my grandfather first knocked on your apartment door."

Marissa was speechless.

"The thing is," Khalid added softly, his focus riveted on the pan, "my father actually came for me. Maybe he felt guilty—or parental, or what, I don't know. He came to the States and found me while I was still young, was granted temporary custody and spent two weeks looking after me. Then he changed his mind and dropped me back off, in the middle of the night, and never came back. Went to California and lived in a hotel in L.A. until he died. Thirty years, just one state away from me all that time."

Her mouth was dry. "Do you remember him?" she managed to ask.

"I was too young to remember any of this. It was all there, though, in my grandfather's files."

"Do you sometimes wish your grandfather had never found you?"

Khalid put down the spatula he'd been staring at so intently and turned to her. "No, I never wish that. Rifaisa is my destiny." He smiled sadly. "You were the one always talking about destiny, remember? You said it was what brought us together." His voice was cold, almost mocking, when he said the words.

"I don't believe in all that anymore," Marissa said, even as she let one hand slide over her stomach unconsciously.

～

KHALID PLATED the omelette he'd made, handed it over to Marissa, wishing he'd never started talking about his family, his father, all that dirty laundry that didn't need to be aired. Back in Vegas, one of the things he'd loved about her was her way of listening that always drew him out. She still had it. She still had a lot for him to love.

Apparently, though, she didn't have the blind faith in the world that everything would turn out how it was supposed to anymore. He frowned. Had he been the one to shatter that, when'd he'd let a rumor drive him away from her?

"Bon appétit," he said, as he poured her a glass of sparkling water and set it before her on the tall counter where she sat.

"Aren't you eating?" she asked. "There's enough here for two, easily. Maybe three."

Khalid narrowed his eyes. "Sorry, no," he said, already backing out of the galley. "I'm needed on the sundeck, with everyone else."

She inclined her head, curiously. "Taking the afternoon off with your staff?" she asked. She looked genuinely surprised. Apparently, she too had decided he was a workaholic.

"Working," he corrected her, and stepped backward. "We get better sat phone reception up there."

She shrugged. "I don't know how anyone can work with the beautiful ocean stretching out in every direction like this."

He responded only with a frown, before he turned and left the galley. He knew what she was thinking but refused to say. He'd started taking all the trappings of his new life for granted. And suddenly he wished he didn't have to. Having her here, watching her look around in wonder at the yacht and the sea and the plane and everything else that came with his job—his *destiny*, as she might have called it all those years ago—was bad for his work ethic. Having her so close by in this damned claustrophobic yacht —a yacht that had seemed more than large enough when he'd first laid eyes on it—was more distracting than he cared to admit.

He needed to get used to it, he told himself. If she were pregnant, this would be his life. Her presence in the palace, slinging barbs at him, looking so goddamned irresistible while she tucked ravenously into an omelette—and then forgetting he existed the moment he was out of sight. He thought of his constant diplomatic trips and groaned, running a hand through his thick black hair in frustration. Would he even be able to leave her behind if he had access to her body in the marital bed? He would be distracted if she were there and distracted if she weren't.

And then there was a piece of him—the piece that had been awakened when she told him about her prior pregnancy—that dared to fantasize about the possibility of a child. He had always imagined he would make a fine father—not that the bar was set very high based on his past experiences. He would enjoy sharing his world with children, hearing them laugh when they saw the peacocks in the garden, teaching them soccer. He just hadn't imagined it would be under these circumstances.

As he began to climb the stairs to the sundeck, his steps grew heavier. He didn't want to try to focus on contracts and negotiations and politics. Those things would do little to distract him from his thoughts of Marissa, of her long fall of dark hair curling around the face that had him so hypnotized. Of how her soft, willing body had felt under his that night in Cairo.

He needed a distraction. A physical distraction, something that would exhaust his body and quiet his mind. He pushed his shoulders up and back and let his head roll around loosely for a moment, discarding the tension that had been building and building since he had laid eyes on her. Then he went to the bridge to deliver a specific set of instructions to his captain. Work would wait.

Within a half an hour they were anchored a hundred meters off Jumeirah beach, along with a dozen or so pleasure boats at the end of their days of cruising and sightseeing around the man-made islands to their west. The sun was still bright, and there would be a few more hours of daylight. Khalid would spend them in the water. He made quick work of changing into surf shorts and headed for the swimming deck at the stern. In minutes he was swimming away the frustrations of his current circumstances, nothing on his mind but water and breath. The sweet, familiar burn in his lungs as he worked harder and harder, swimming out first in the creases the waves made, and then bodysurfing his way back to the yacht. It was heaven, the sun low enough in the sky to turn the waves into piles of diamonds, but still warm enough to evaporate the droplets on his forehead each time he stopped to catch his breath. He had no idea how long he was out, but when the sun began to color the sky a rich orange, he knew it was time to turn in. Finally he felt still, quiet, calm. He drank in the sensation as he swam back for the swimming deck at a leisurely pace, taking deeper and deeper breaths, cooling his body down.

An effort that was wasted when he saw what was waiting for him.

Wearing nothing more than what seemed to be a length of butcher's twine with a few squares of white fabric over her breasts and a long towel wrapped around her waist, her hair loose over the pale white skin of her shoulders, a mermaid appeared to be sitting on the deck of his ship. But no, it was a human woman hanging her ankles into the sea and watching him intently. Her body was real, as were her long, creamy-colored legs that dangled absently in the water and her full, rounded breasts, only a scrap of cloth away from his hands. From his mouth.

He groaned and felt himself stir below. It seemed he would be staying in the water a little longer than he'd planned—at least until he could get control of himself. He swam to the deck and used one strong arm to wrap around the ladder and hold himself steady as he looked up at her. But the close-up view of that bikini —barely thick enough to cover the buds of pink nipples that cried out for his tongue—only made the desire grow stronger.

"Thinking of a swim?" he called, hearing the thickness of his voice. Watching her lick her lower lip in unconscious response.

"I was. But I changed my mind when I saw that the water was already occupied."

He smiled despite himself. "I would hope the Persian Gulf would be big enough for the two of us."

She looked away, saying nothing in reply. Maybe she was thinking the same thing as him—that even this vast expanse of water might feel small when shared between them.

The thought of it heated him. Made him want her more than ever. "Get in," he called up to her. He let go of the ladder and swam closer to where she sat. He knew he shouldn't, but he did it anyway.

"I like it up here. From above, I can almost see all of your ego." She jutted out her chin with defiance. That little action pushed him over the edge.

"My ego would like you in here," he said, his voice now little more than a growl. His mind, and his reason, had disappeared into the rolling waves. All that was left was lust.

"I don't think so," she said, but her words were halting. Hesitant.

"Then I will persuade you." And with the words, he reached for her calf. Brought it up in his hands, and caressed it softly, luxuriating in the sensation of her smooth, strong legs. And then without any hint of what he was about to do next, surprising even himself, he pressed his lips to the ball of her foot, dragged upward, and then slipped her big toe inside his mouth with a groan.

MARISSA LEANED BACK on the swimming deck with a gasp. She'd watched him swimming for so long, she'd forgotten that he would eventually come back in. And when he did, his dark skin cutting through the blue-green ocean, the muscles of his back hypnotizing her, she'd forgotten where she was. Forgotten he would see her watching him. Forgotten that when he wanted her, she was powerless to turn him away even after everything.

And he wanted her now. His tongue ran a circle around her toe, then retreated, then made its lazy loop again, making every inch of her foot feel as though it were electrified, sending waves of current into her body, up her legs to the core of her. His mouth hot from the sun and the exertion, his kiss seemed to burn a path across the pad of each toe, as he took one after another into his mouth and swirled it with his tongue, and then he moved his attentions to the curve of her instep, using his lips to rub and nibble at the sensitive skin there, while she did nothing but lean back on her hands and sigh with pleasure. It was too much to ask that she stop him. What he did to her made her lose control. And the wicked look in his eyes told her that he knew it.

When her left foot was covered in kisses, he lowered it back, trailing his hands up her calf and under the sarong she had tucked around her waist as cover-up, untying it, revealing the somewhat scandalous bikini she had found wrapped prettily in a box on her bed earlier. She'd believe it a thoughtful gesture on his part. Now she saw his ulterior motive. And she couldn't seem to make herself care. Not while he was running his fingers down her other calf and repeating his teasing licks and kisses every step of the way. When her right foot was as well attended to as her left, he pushed her feet together, grabbed her by the thighs, and pulled her into the water with him. There was a splash as her body entered the warm water, and she clung to him as she got used to the feeling of lightness and wetness. And then, as she hung off his hard body, he took her mouth in a sun-warmed kiss, the kiss she hadn't known she needed. But she did, desperately.

Like a misplaced key finally finding the right lock, his kiss undid her. The passion of it traveled down her spine and liquefied her core, leaving her mindless with desire. The long kiss was followed by another and another, each deeper and more desperate, until he broke his mouth away and said, "At this rate, we'll both be drowned in minutes." He pushed her up against the ladder, hard enough that it gave her a little shock, and she wound her arms up through the handles and held on for dear life.

In minutes he was free of his shorts, and pressing his hard shaft at her bikini-clad entrance insistently. She did nothing at all to restrain him, instead tilting her pelvis upward slightly to give him an easier vantage. He took it, pressing aside the thin fabric to thrust into her, and she gasped as the feeling of fullness and stretching abated, returned, and abated again. Holding onto the back of the ladder with one hand, Khalid used the other to reach between them, pressing his thumb over her most sensitive stretch of flesh, moving in rhythm to his thrusts.

Faster than she ever thought possible, she felt the vibrations moving into her, pushing through her stronger and stronger. She screamed noiselessly, then moaned his name, letting the shock and bliss run through every inch of her body as she came. She felt his body grow rigid, his thrusts grow more insistent, and heard a guttural growl from deep within him. Eventually, they were both still, their bodies limp in the bobbing ocean, the waves tracing a line over her sensitized nipples.

Her arms began to ache from clinging to the ladder. She shifted slightly, moving to ease the strain, and he moved too, slipped out of her and to the side. Then, using one hand braced against the deck to hold them both, he scooped her under her legs and let her lie there, one arm over his shoulders, weightless and exhausted.

They floated there, soundless, for a very long time. Then he spoke. "Well, I suppose the damage is done by now."

"Would it be so bad?" she whispered, imagining the baby she'd lost, and the one she might be carrying now, especially if they kept sleeping together without birth control.

Khalid didn't answer. And his silence was deafening.

8

KHALID'S WORDS—AND HIS SILENCE—STAYED WITH MARISSA FOR THE rest of the night. She ruminated over their conversation while the whole group ate dinner at a long glass table positioned on the uppermost deck, under an awning with a stunning view of the water and Dubai's marina in three directions. She thought of them still when she went to bed, alone, in her small stateroom, just a short hallway away from his. There hadn't been a chance to ask that he answer her question—they'd had to scuttle out of the water and to their separate cabins to avoid being seen by one of the yacht's plentiful crew. But Marissa was able to speculate what his answer would be. They'd just inadvertently doubled their chances of a pregnancy.

And Khalid thought they were idiots for doing so.

And yet the thoughts of their lovemaking—and not regretful thoughts, either—kept Marissa awake late into the night. Those thoughts tortured her mind the next day, when she awoke to find that they'd made it to Rifaisa. The thoughts chased her off the yacht and into the limousine that waited to usher the entire party to the palace.

Only when they pulled into the long, long drive, past booths of guards, through gate after gate, and the palace came into view, did she think about anything else. The royal residence was magnificent, but nothing like what she'd expected. It was large but not enormous, and it seemed to be relatively recent construction—perhaps in the last hundred years at the outside. Three large sets of pillars rose to a striking angled roof in front, but they were the only nod to historical architecture. Behind them were walls of windows and vast stretches of verandas that wrapped around the high second story almost like on an old American plantation home.

Khalid must have seen the surprise on her face, because he laughed at her as they both slid out of the car. "Were you expecting the Taj Mahal?" he asked her.

Marissa made a face at him. "Maybe I was. But this will do," she laughed back, happy for even a moment of lightness between them. "The grounds are spectacular."

All around them were modern fountains, set to spray at a series of different heights that gave them an almost architectural feel, as if the walls of water were just another room in the palace. She longed to explore them more and see the exotic flowers that seemed to bloom around every corner.

"Wait until you see the orchard," Khalid replied. "But the tour will have to wait. I'm behind a day in my schedule and will have to make it all up today. Tomorrow we're expected in the north."

"What do you mean, *we're* expected?" Marissa asked, following him up the path and between the pillars.

He stopped, only for a second. "I mean, until we know what is going on down there," with his words he pointed at Marissa's belly like it was a bomb that could go off, "I'm not letting you out of my sight. I have business in the north. You'll come along and try to stay out of the way."

Marissa's eyes widened at the admonishment, and she

couldn't hold her tongue. "I tried to stay out of your way on the yacht," she said, lowering her voice so no one else could hear. "And look where that got us."

Khalid was still walking to the palace as she spoke, so she couldn't see the expression on his face when she'd brought up what they'd done in the water the night before. But she didn't need to see him to know her words had angered him. He let out a low growl and stormed into an enormous, open hall that stretched out in every direction and soared up to the palace's ceiling. Then he pivoted on her, and the intensity in his eyes was as startling as the beauty of the room.

"We'll discuss that later," he hissed. "*In private.*"

She opened her mouth to argue, but changed her mind when his staff appeared.

"For now, follow Jana." He said, waving dismissively. "She'll see that you're settled, and give you the lay of the land. I've got work to do, and she does too, so try not to keep her long. There's a library, and wifi, and a pool. You shouldn't be bored."

She nodded. "I may not rule an entire nation, your majesty, but I do have my own work to catch up on."

"Fine," he echoed, beginning to walk away but then stopping himself to add a final thought. "If you decide to swim, ask a maid to find you something suitable. I don't want to see that bikini again. It's counterproductive."

Marissa felt her cheeks catch fire. "But you gave it to me."

He was already walking away, leaving her fuming. How good he had gotten at cutting her down with just a few words. She thought of the things he'd said to her over the course of the last four days, and for the first time since this whole affair had started, she let herself get truly angry. So he found her "counterproductive." Apparently she was getting in the way of his schedule. Well, then, maybe he shouldn't have kissed her! Maybe he shouldn't have pulled her into the sea with him. Maybe he shouldn't have abandoned her in America without so much as a goodbye before marrying some *Rifaisi social climber!* Talk about counterproductive.

Marissa looked to her left and right and found she was, once again, surrounded by people. Her familiar bodyguard from the hotel headed her way, as did Jana. She wished she could scream. She wished she could rush after him and give him the good hard shove he deserved. She wished, more than any of those things, that she could bolt out the door, run like hell to the nearest airport, and get away from this damned country she'd never asked to visit.

But instead she took a very deep breath. She pushed down all the rage, tried to wipe the grimace off her face, composed herself as best she could, and smiled at the approaching aide. Things, she reminded herself, would surely get worse before they got better. She'd have to save her emotional energy if she wanted to get through what lay ahead.

She'd need every last drop of willpower in the coming days if she had any hope of keeping her head on straight and her heart intact.

THE NEXT MORNING, before the sun had made it very high in the sky, Khalid slipped out of his bedroom onto the expansive balcony that rounded the entire rear of the palace. Taking his coffee out here had become something of a ritual for him, a moment of perfect peace and privacy every day before he stepped into his role as leader and statesman. He cherished it, cherished the view of the beautiful date orchards and the sea stretching out behind it, and off to the south, the busy port already bustling with enormous tankers making their way to the mouth of the gulf. As long as there was peace in his country and that port was busy, he knew he was doing his job well. Normally, that thought satisfied him well enough.

But today, he was unsatisfied.

He looked down the long expanse of balcony to the farthest end, where she sat, perched on a teak bench working on her own cup of coffee. She took it with enough milk to turn it a pale shade of tan, he remembered, and without a grain of sugar. He hoped his staff had gotten it right this morning.

Then he wondered why on earth he cared.

He'd noticed her presence the moment he'd stepped outside, almost as though he'd felt, rather than seen, her. But she remained oblivious, staring out toward the port as though she understood just how important it was to the people around her. If she enjoyed this view, maybe she wouldn't hate living here as much as he'd always assumed. Maybe she'd even come to like it over time. He supposed that would be for the best—life would be easier if his wife wasn't miserable. If he did, in fact, have to make her his wife.

But he was fooling himself to think she could bear it here. She would be miserable. She'd miss her family. Family was everything to Marissa. And though he had no doubt she would make a good mother, he also knew she would make a terrible wife. One he would never be able to trust—one, he wouldn't *let* himself trust.

Khalid shook his head. What did it matter, one wife or another? His last attempt at matrimony had been a sham, but that sham had produced no heirs. So even if Marissa were pregnant, and he had to marry her, he supposed it would be no different than what he'd already done for the sake of his country.

Only it was different. Very different. While Nuriyah had been beautiful and charming and seductive in her own heavy-handed way, Marissa was something altogether unique. She had a way of turning him on even without trying, and when they were together, he could think of nothing else but her. It was the residue of an immature first love, he told himself, but deep inside he wondered if the connection between them was something more than that. Their lovemaking was unlike anything he'd felt with any other woman. And try as he might, he couldn't explain it away.

Nor could he resist her, he thought with a silent groan, wishing even now that he could go to her, pull that mug of coffee out of her hands and lead her into her own chambers, which lay through a door just inches from where she now stood, leaning against the balcony railing. If she were pregnant with his child, there would be that one silver lining—unlimited access to her bed. For he knew she wanted him, too, even if she wished to be anywhere else but here. When he touched her, he saw it in her eyes, that frisson of desire that stoked his own fires more.

There was no missing that want in her face. That look of need. And the need was mutual.

Exasperated, Khalid set his coffee on the thick stone balcony and turned, strode toward her, steeling himself for that look, mounting his resistance.

"Marissa," he barked. He enjoyed watching her jump slightly when she heard him. She spun around, pulling up the long, loosely woven grey wrap that had slipped down on her shoulders.

"Good morning," she said. "I was just watching the activity down at the ports."

He rose his eyebrows. "It's the heart of this city. I'll take you down there and show you around so you can see the workings of it. If it turns out you'll be living here—"

"About that," she interrupted slowly, great hesitance in her voice. "If it turns out I'm, we're, pregnant, what would you think of me traveling back and forth between Las Vegas and here? So the baby could know both sides of his family, and so I wouldn't be so alone?"

"Absolutely not," he declared, folding his arms to make it

clear he was unwilling to discuss the matter further. "Your family can travel here if they want to spend time with the baby. The *hypothetical* baby. It's too dangerous for you and the heir to Rifaisa to travel. Too costly to protect you."

Marissa started to protest, but he held his hand up, dismissing her protests. "Enough. Go get ready to travel. We're expected in time for lunch in the northlands."

"I am ready," she shot back. "I just need to put on a sweater."

He looked her up and down, noticing her outfit for the first time since he'd seen her on the balcony. Under the wrap she wore a silky tank that exposed her arms and a long, soft-looking camel-colored skirt that glanced off her hips. A black headscarf partially covered her curls. She looked elegant and utterly appropriate for the less cosmopolitan region they were about to visit, but for her bare arms. He frowned. "I suppose that will do," he said gruffly. He began to turn away from her, to return to his own chambers, but she grabbed him suddenly by the arm.

"I can dress myself, Khalid," she told him through clenched teeth. "This situation is hard enough for me without this imperious act of yours. That's not who you are. I know you. We were in love once. Treat me with the respect that deserves."

He rolled his shoulder, yanked his arm out of her reach, irritated. She didn't know him anymore. And he didn't know her. But she was right about one thing. They had been in love. And it was an experience he didn't care to repeat. "In Rifaisa, respect is earned, Marissa," he uttered. "Earned. Not given."

THE MOMENT she stepped into her chambers Marissa let out her frustration in a scream. She knew he could probably hear it out on the balcony, knew that the guard positioned just outside her bedroom door could hear it too. And didn't care. She couldn't think of another time in her life she'd been this frustrated. And not just frustrated with her circumstances, or with Khalid. Frustrated with herself.

For when he'd snuck up on her this morning she'd been looking out at the beautiful landscape around her and daydreaming about living here. At the palace. Like a little girl caught up in a princess fantasy, too young to understand that sometimes the fairy-tale prince might have a heart of ice.

There was a knock at the door. "Ms. Madden?" she heard a male voice say in a thick Arabic accent. "Ms. Madden?" he repeated.

She went to the door and opened it, seeing her bodyguard there, looking concerned. She smiled at him, nodded and gestured around to show that she was fine. He smiled back broadly and stepped out, closing the door behind him courteously, and she marveled at how kindly people were treating her, even though she was a stranger who couldn't speak one word of the language. They showed her respect from the word go, she thought. It was only Khalid who was making her work for it.

Still seething, she pulled on her thin navy cotton cardigan, leaving the buttons undone to keep it from hugging her curves too tightly, and grabbed her overnight bag. Jana had warned her that this time of year weather in the desert could be uncertain, and it was better to plan for delays and be pleased when none presented themselves. There was a metaphor there, Marissa was sure. Plan to be cut down by Khalid, and then she would just be pleasantly surprised if he was nice to her. She frowned. She could live with that for a few weeks, sure. But certainly not for a lifetime.

She made her way down to the palace's great hall, where Amid and Jana slowly explained their travel plans to her in English. They would travel to the residence of an important sheikh whose lands included a strip of beach Khalid wanted to convert into a protected national park. Mostly it would be a diplomatic trip, lots of smiling and politeness. She would be introduced as a college friend of Khalid's who was here to visit the country and see its most beautiful sights—including the beach.

"Mr. Abbasi will explain the politics of the situation in more detail in the car," Jana added, and Marissa couldn't miss the slightest quirk of a frown on Amid's face at the words. He had certainly been the least friendly of all the staff she'd met up to now, but that didn't bother her. He was protective, she suspected.

She was herded into the passenger seat of a Range Rover, where she waited for only a moment before Khalid appeared, still clicking through emails on his mobile phone even as he buckled his seat belt in the driver's seat.

"You're driving?" she exclaimed, surprised to see him there.

"I'm allowed to drive a car. After all, I am a prince."

She quirked a brow. "I just didn't realize you could set down your laptop and phones long enough to steer."

He started the car and put it into gear. "I've found it works better if I do. Especially with a stick shift." They pulled out of the drive and began to head out of the city. After a few moments of silence, he started pointing out sights, almost as though he couldn't help himself.

"That's the turn that leads to the port," he said at a busy intersection. "And you can see from the traffic that it's very much the hub of the city."

Marissa was interested in learning about Rifaisa. But she was so tired of Khalid's mercurial treatment of her that she couldn't bring herself to speak to him.

He continued, though, without her encouragement. "All of the oil tankers are taxed and serviced by my people. Those taxes fund our schools, which are top-notch and—for the last fifteen years—bilingual. It's why you are finding it so easy to communicate."

She stared straight ahead, silent. His words from that morning —respect must be *earned*—churning through her head.

"Learning both English and Arabic gives us a leg up in industry and other areas, like banking," he added. "And in addition the oil companies pay us hefty fees for what we call the Environmental Impact Adjustment. To make up for all the carbon they use and the pollutants that more often than not make their way into the gulf. That funds an enormous CO_2 storage project offshore, as well as the water cleanup that keeps the sea safe and healthy. And creates endless jobs for Rifaisis."

Her eyes widened, at this final bit of information, impressed that his small region had found a profitable way to be caretakers of the earth.

Khalid turned to her for a moment. "It will be a long drive if you refuse to speak."

She laughed bitterly. "You're allowed to ice me out whenever you see fit, but I don't have the same right to sit in silence after you mistreat me?"

"I hardly mistreated you."

"You forbade me from visiting my home."

There was a moment's pause. When he spoke again, Khalid's tone was softer. "That was rash. Surely you realize I'd let you spend time with your family. I'm not a monster."

With that, Marissa's temper boiled over. "Surely I know? Surely I did not know. You may not be a monster, but I'm definitely not a mind reader. I only know what you say to me. And I take what you say to me seriously. If you say I can't see my family, or say I don't deserve respect—when I may be carrying your child—I will take that seriously."

He was silent.

"Well?" she demanded.

"I believe I can see your point," he said at last. "I will temper my rhetoric."

"Good idea," Marissa snapped in reply. "Maybe you'll find that if you temper your rhetoric, I'll temper my, well, temper."

"Agreed," said Khalid. "Now, if the air is clear, perhaps I could resume my endless lecturing on the main exports and gross national product of Rifaisa?"

Marissa exhaled. "Well, fine. I must admit I'm interested. And besides, you do seem very passionate on this subject."

"I am. As heir, it's all up to me—for my grandfather still manages much of the old-school politics—to be a steward for the future."

"It seems like you're doing a good job, if all these green jobs you talk about are coming to fruition."

"And Madden Construction?" he asked. "Is it satisfying work?"

"Satisfying, yes," Marissa conceded. "Passion-inducing, though? Not yet."

Khalid made a soft sound of understanding. "Passion counts for a lot."

Maybe too much, thought Marissa.

For a little while, they were both silent. After a while, when they made it outside the city, Khalid began again to point out landmarks. Clearly, he couldn't resist the subject. He told her about the red dunes she would soon see, the harshness of life between cities in this barren land, and the surprising amount of wildlife to be found within the desert expanses. As he talked, Marissa watched the landscape grow more and more foreboding, the roads grow more treacherous, and felt the age of the place she was in, the mystery it held.

He was quite the expert on the country—obviously he had studied its natural and political history with the same vigor that he'd always brought to his work, only now it was much, much more personal than any job he'd had before. His eyes seemed lit from within as he pointed out first one thing, then another. He wove stories of the warring sheikhs who had laid wreckage to the area and then left, declaring it too foreboding. His own distant ancestors had pressed through the desert a thousand years ago and found the gleaming beaches and one perfectly shaped cove, yet unclaimed, ripe for a port. He told her of his grandfather's epic love for the daughter of a rival sheikh that had brought a lasting peace to the area for the past sixty years, even after her death.

The stories made the travel pass, and when the neighboring sheikh's gardens came into sight, Marissa looked at her watch in wonder. "Is this it already?" she asked.

"This is it. The oasis of Sheikh al Fulan. Let me get your door."

The moment their feet hit the heavily landscaped earth, they quickly became caught up in introductions and greetings. She met the sheikh they had come to see, his various aides, and countless family members, who all greeted her warmly, if slightly curiously. They were sent up to luxurious rooms and left alone to clean up for lunch. They all reconvened in an elaborate dining room laden with *mezze*, small dishes of spreads and vegetables that each looked more delicious than the last. Marissa felt her stomach rumble at the sight. She was ready to dig in when the French doors of the dining room sprang open and a woman appeared, tall and stunning and dressed to impress in a long bias-cut silk dress and a diaphanous matching scarf wrapped around her head and neck. Her arms were heavy with gold bracelets. She looked familiar.

Their host stood. Khalid and the other men did as well. Marissa knew at once this was no assistant here to announce an important phone call. "Nuriyah!" the host exclaimed and then added something further in Arabic to the rest of the table, who nodded and smiled. Then he gestured at Marissa and switched to English. "Ms. Madden, my daughter, Nuriyah. Nuriyah, meet Khalid's university friend from America."

Nuriyah. The name clicked into place, and Marissa leaned back in her chair as if blown by a great wind. So this was the sheikh's daughter. Khalid's ex-wife.

She nodded to Marissa and ran to kiss her father's cheek adoringly, before she turned to Khalid. "I hope you don't mind," she said in perfect English. "It was the only day I could make it up to see my family, with my busy schedule in the city. And when Father said you'd be our guest, I thought it would be great to catch up!" She was breathless and wide-eyed. Beautiful.

Khalid reached over to take her hand politely. "Always a pleasure," he said with a smile that seemed genuine.

Nuriyah took the empty seat directly opposite Khalid—right next to Marissa, so that she could feel the thousand-watt smile coming off of her through the entire meal. They were probably playing footsie under the table, she thought with a jealous pang. While the mother of his child—*maybe*—sat just inches away, trying to concentrate on a plate of *taramosalata*.

Wait, Marissa thought. *You're being ridiculous.* Rather than get stuck in some jealous frenzy, she turned to Nuriyah and asked her about her work in PR, and began a conversation with her about marketing that was as friendly as could be. Nuriyah was a perfectly nice person, and a fine conversational partner, and though Marissa would have noticed they had differing interests even if Khalid hadn't already told her so, there was nothing wrong with her mind. The woman was intelligent and knew what she wanted from life, thought Marissa. She would never have let Khalid tell her what to do or where she could or couldn't go, no matter the circumstances. No wonder they'd split up so quickly. Marissa realized that under the right circumstances, she and Nuriyah might have become friends.

After dinner the group moved to a beautiful poolside patio, where they found three little girls making the most of the large shallow pool, especially the fountain of water that sprayed over into it and caused endless opportunities for splashes and squeals. As the adults sat and drank a strong bitter tea unlike anything

Marissa had ever tasted, she watched the children's antics with amusement, while Khalid and the sheikh settled into low-toned private conversation.

"They're my nieces," said Nuriyah, gesturing to the pool as she slipped so gracefully into the seat nearest Marissa's. "Daughters of my older sister."

"Adorable girls," Marissa commented.

"Aren't they?" Nuriyah replied, pride in her voice. "This is the best way to enjoy children, I think, as an auntie. I get all the holidays and happy occasions. But when they cry, it's not my problem."

"Opting against having children must be difficult here." Marissa gestured at Nuriyah's father.

"It's certainly frowned upon in our culture, but my father supports me. He has plenty of grandchildren now." Nuriyah examined Marissa. "Do you want children of your own, Marissa?"

"I do. Someday." With those words, Marissa finally admitted to herself what she had been afraid to face for the last several days: A part of her hoped she was pregnant. She certainly didn't want to be stuck in a marriage with a man who drove her mad with desire and frustration at the same time. But did she want to be a mother? Oh, yes. She had wanted it three years ago, but she'd been afraid to face trying again after she'd lost the baby. She'd been too petrified to even dream of motherhood.

Now, if she were in fact pregnant, it would be a fait accompli. The decision would have been made for her, and she would have to stare down the fears she had developed since the accident. She would have no choice. Only now she would be facing them much more alone than she'd imagined. With a man who couldn't love her by her side.

As though she could read minds, Nuriyah turned her head to Khalid and laughed. "I'm sure he's told you that's why we didn't work out," she said lightly, with a tip of the head toward her ex-husband. "Our differing views on children."

Marissa said nothing, shocked by Nuriyah's frankness.

"It's too bad," Nuriyah went on. "Everything else was so good, if you know what I mean." She winked, and Marissa felt her stomach tighten. "They just don't make men like him every day. But he wants a family, and I don't. We simply weren't in the cards. Who knows what the cards hold for you."

Marissa paled. The conversation had turned too personal. Too quickly. She suddenly rose to her feet. "The sun," she said, feeling ridiculous since they were sitting in the thin shade of a patio umbrella. "I think I've gotten too much sun." Luckily, she was so flushed from stress she felt sure it would look as though she were developing a sunburn, despite the thick coat of sunscreen she'd wiped on that morning.

Nuriyah stood too and put the back of her hand to Marissa's flaming cheek. "You poor thing. Let me take you to my room and make you a compress."

Marissa forced a grateful smile, but all she wanted was to escape this conversation. Then, out of nowhere, Khalid's voice cut in.

"Ladies," he said, approaching from where he'd been sitting with Nuriyah's father. His eyes were locked on Marissa in a way that made her swallow hard. "It's getting later in the day, and I promised Marissa a trip to see the beaches. She studied marine biology in school, did she tell you?"

Marissa tried not to choke as he delivered such an outlandish lie.

"She didn't mention it," said Nuriyah, not hiding her skepticism. "Such a departure from corporate marketing."

Khalid shrugged. "She's full of surprises," he said dismissively. "Would you mind lending her a shade umbrella? She's looking a little flushed. Sun getting to you, Marissa?"

She nodded, still not daring to speak a word.

"Of course," said Nuriyah. "If you'll give us a moment, we can all go down together."

Khalid shook his head. "Not necessary. Stay here, enjoy the pool and your beautiful little nieces. I know how you love children, and you have such little free time to visit, as you said."

Marissa gave Nuriyah a look over her shoulder as Khalid led her away. Khalid hardly seemed to notice. He was already slipping his arm in Marissa's, calling to a pair of nearby bodyguards that it was time to go.

9

Khalid wasn't sure exactly why he'd rushed to Marissa's aid when he'd seen her getting upset while talking to Nuriyah. He figured Nuriyah had said something to upset her, as Nuriyah had often infuriated him, and he wanted to dash to Marissa's rescue. After Marissa had blistered him with her words in the trip up here, he wanted her to look at him with kindness again. Damn it, he wanted to earn her smile.

But as they bumped along in the Range Rover, navigating the sand and gravel trails that were the only way to reach the isolated beaches, he saw no smile. Just trepidation. Damn that wide-eyed face of hers.

"What's wrong, Marissa?"

"Why did you do that?" she asked. Of course she couldn't leave any subject unspoken. Of course he loved that about her.

"Do what?"

"Rescue me from Nuriyah?"

Khalid laughed at her choice of words. "First you tell me you could raise a baby all on your own, and now you need rescuing from a meek Rifaisi woman?"

"She's hardly meek, as you surely know. And I didn't need

rescuing from her, exactly. I needed rescuing from the thought of a loveless marriage."

Khalid said nothing. If only she could know how much the opposite frightened him.

"So tell me, once and for all," Marissa pressed on. "Why did you show me that small kindness? Why did you lie to Nuriyah, desert your meeting, and whisk me away?"

Khalid lightened his foot on the gas as the road grew more and more uneven. He noticed that she was gripping the door handle tightly, but somehow managed to keep the rest of her body loose. She was a natural at off-road travel, he thought curiously. Lucky for her. Aside from the city and the major thoroughfares, the roads in Rifaisa were catch as catch can. There would be a lot of bumpy travel if they were married. Every day would be as off-kilter as this one.

"I lied to her because I can," he said, deciding not to divulge these disorienting feelings until he could better understand them for himself. "It's one of the perks of being a prince. I'm never wrong."

Marissa looked at him hard. Then she seemed to let the subject go. "You're wrong all the time," she shot back. "It's just that no one has the guts to tell you so."

"Lucky I have you here, then, wouldn't you say?"

Marissa practically growled, but there was good humor in his voice. "Lucky for you. Not so lucky for me."

He laughed, and finally, finally, he realized the true reason he'd pulled her away today. Because he'd wanted to be alone with her. *Would it be so bad?* she'd asked him. And he was beginning to think maybe it would not.

"Anyway," he said quickly, hoping she hadn't noticed the flicker of recognition on his face, "I was ready to go to the beach, and I thought it was better if you were with me, rather than left to be interrogated by the old sheikh and his daughters. They'd have you confessing to our situation in minutes. And where would that leave me?"

Even with his eyes focused on the road, he could feel Marissa staring at him for a long time after he spoke, probably trying to read him, figure out if he were telling the truth. Which of course he wasn't. At last she exhaled, and he found he too had been holding his breath. "You're probably right," she said. "All they would have needed to do is threaten me with more of that awful tea."

"You mean *qat*? You didn't drink it, did you?"

"I couldn't take more than a tiny sip," she said. "I've never tasted anything like it. Thankfully."

"That's because you can't get it in the States. It's a narcotic. Thank goodness you didn't drink much. It can't be good for the baby." As soon as the words were out, he wanted to smack himself. "The hypothetical baby," he amended.

But it was too late. He'd already given away his own mind. Now she had to know that part of him was wishing for the baby.

Marissa cleared her throat. "Maybe it's time we think of a better term than 'hypothetical baby,'" she said, her voice as relaxed as her body despite the uncertain terrain. "We may know within the week. The tests they have now are much faster than the ones they had even three years ago."

"How do you know that?" he asked.

"I've been doing some research online. I also discovered that over-the-counter pregnancy tests aren't available in Rifaisa."

"We're a progressive enclave with an American-born prince, but we're still smack dab in the middle of the Arabian Peninsula. It's why I work so closely with both Jana and Amid. She is the most qualified, but much of my business takes me places where she simply cannot attend."

She nodded. "Even so, it's a predicament in terms of finding out the situation while maintaining our privacy."

"Is your period reliable?"

She laughed, and Khalid couldn't resist sneaking a peek from the road to catch that glimmer that made its way to her bright eyes. "Think of the scandal if the old sheikh could hear us now! But yes, yes, it's pretty much clockwork. It's just that stress has a way of knocking a woman off-kilter. And I have been under a bit of stress."

He twisted his lips. He had been a little heavy-handed with her. But then, this was the same woman who had concealed her first pregnancy.

"If you're late," he said with conviction, "even by a day, we'll speak to my personal doctor. I trust him to be discreet. At least long enough to make arrangements."

"Arrangements for a wedding, you mean." Her voice sounded shaky. "Couldn't there be some other way?"

Khalid's shoulders slumped. "Unless you're willing to leave the baby here and sign away your maternal rights?"

She gasped. "No!"

"That's what I thought. Then no. I am already once divorced. There is only so much the people will tolerate. If you bear my child, you will be my wife." He hated the way the words sounded on his lips. Almost like a life sentence. He stole another glance away from the road and saw that all the earlier sparkle had gone out of her eyes. She looked utterly defeated.

"I'm sorry this is happening, Marissa," he said, forcing his own frustration out of his voice. "I know it's not what you want."

She sighed, a big motion that caused her shoulders to rise and fall slowly. "I'm scared, Khalid."

"Scared?" It took a moment for him to understand what she meant. When he did, a twinge of sadness passed over him. "Because of what happened the last time?"

"Yes. If I am pregnant, how will I keep the baby safe? What if something happens?"

Khalid cut her off, unwilling to let her put herself through the doubt, the recrimination no one deserved. Without thinking, he let his hand slip to her knee reassuringly. "Let that be my concern. I will keep you and the baby safe."

Marissa looked down at the spot where his hand touched the fabric of her skirt and fell silent, as if she were drinking in his words. Then she looked up at him, her round eyes shining. "It's not how I imagined it," she said at last. "But if I am—if we are pregnant, I will be happy to be a mother."

Khalid paused for a moment, then decided there was no harm in admitting the truth. She'd get it out of him eventually anyway. "Me too. A father, I mean."

"Even if the child is mine?"

Khalid looked for the words he needed. "It wouldn't have to be a completely loveless marriage," he began. "I mean, in time, it might be possible for us to…" His voice trailed off.

Marissa jumped on his words. "Do you think?"

Before he could even hear the end of what he knew was an impossible question, he heard the annoying beep of his radio.

"What was that?" she asked.

"It's the other car trying to reach us. There's a handheld in the glove box."

"A walkie-talkie?" she asked as she fished it out.

"We don't get much cell service out here," he quipped, then took it from her and depressed the speak button. "Abbasi."

"Sir, we're getting word of bad weather coming. Nothing serious, but we shouldn't stay at the beach too long."

Khalid looked out at the skies. It looked like nothing more than a beautiful late afternoon. Bright blue skies, and the creamy white beach finally within sight. He groaned. He'd hoped to have time to explore the site of his prospective park and still make it home to the city tonight.

"Right, thanks," he barked back and set down the radio. "We'll have to cut this short," he told Marissa. "But still, you have to see this beach. It's the most beautiful place in the world."

HE WASN'T EXAGGERATING, even in the slightest. At five p.m., with the sun starting to lower in the sky, the rocky shores were glinting and bouncing the light in every direction, making the sand look like it glowed. There were clouds, way off on the horizon, but other than that it was ideal beach weather, and the spray of the waves offered relief from the heat. The tide was going out, she saw, leaving behind a beautiful pattern of rippled sand and rock polished over centuries. Standing several yards back from the water, where she was well clear of getting damp feet, Marissa bent and lifted up one perfectly round white stone, slid her fingers over it, and turned it over in her hand. It felt like glass.

Khalid waved her over and began to lead her down the beach, to where the crags of rock extended further into the water, cutting off their path. Behind them, the bodyguards trailed discreetly, but there was no forgetting they were there. Marissa was starting to feel the burden of never being alone. Again she marveled that Khalid could manage this life, after growing up so very much on his own.

After they'd walked as far as they could, each commenting on the beauty of the area or its possibilities from time to time, but mostly moving ahead in a companionable silence, they sat down on a low constellation of rocks that had been exposed by the retreating tide. As they watched the sun sink lower in the sky, Marissa let her mind wander to thoughts of the future. She could see that this would make a wonderful national park. Khalid had mentioned he thought it would be best accessed by boat, which would allow them to closely regulate the number of visitors and limit the intrusions they caused, but still allow citizens to experience this place of unique beauty. It was an inspired idea. She knew from her own travels that every time she saw the beauty of nature at a park or protected wilderness, she was that much more motivated to do everything she could to preserve it for future generations. Maybe someday, her own child would get to sail up to this magnificent beach and see it in almost the exact same condition as she saw it now—not as an overdeveloped resort or littered wasteland.

Lulled by the soft sounds of the waves, she let herself imagine such a day, slipping out of the self-protective mind-set she'd been wrapped in so tightly, if only for a moment. A family holiday, she, Khalid, and their child—or maybe children?—making a day trip, exploring the beach together and laughing at the antics of the skipjacks and seabirds. She could picture it perfectly, the whole family side by side, and then back on the yacht, the children tucked in bed, and she and Khalid alone together, able to enjoy each other without reservation. To lose themselves in each other's passion. For a lifetime.

Get real, she told herself. It wasn't going to happen. The happy family tableau in her mind was no different than the oasis conjured up by a man dying of thirst in the desert. An illusion.

But for a moment, as they sat quietly side by side, staring out at the endless sea, it seemed like it could be real.

A bird overhead shrieked, and coming back to the present, Marissa felt motion on her shoulder. She turned to face Khalid and saw him looking back at her, bemused. All at once she realized that she had been leaning up against him, using his body to prop up her own while she'd been daydreaming. She sat up with a start, feeling the strange loss that came every time their bodies were separated hit her like a blast of cold air. Khalid merely shook his head and smiled sadly. It had been a long time since she'd seen that faraway look in his eyes. Had he been thinking of a similar future, she wondered, as they'd sat there for who knows how long?

And if he had, then didn't that mean that maybe they had a chance at a marriage that wasn't loveless?

She tried not to let herself consider it, but it was too late. The seed of hope had been planted. Maybe, in time, she could forgive him for leaving her so alone in Las Vegas for such a stupid reason. Not just forgive him—she was well on her way there already, despite her best attempts—but also forget the pain he'd added to the pool of grief she'd already been drowning in from the loss of their unborn child. Maybe they could find a way to develop a real marriage, not one based on an accidental pregnancy, but on more, on the trust and faith in each other that they once had shared. She felt the twinge of her heart as she thought of it. Could she ever again trust him, after what had happened when he left her the first time? She knew it was most likely impossible. But let herself hope, all the same.

"It's time," he said softly, cutting through the swirl of emotions that had begun to engulf her. "We should start our trip home."

The sun was dipping lower, turning the sea a darker blue and the sky into a riot of orange. The tide had moved out quite a long way as they'd been sitting there, revealing more and more of those undulating patterns of sand and rock that Marissa found so beautiful. The sound of the waves was distant now. She nodded. "It's time to go back." She couldn't let herself use the word "home" to describe the palace. Not yet.

Khalid turned to his guards and spoke something to them in Arabic, giving them an accompanying wave that sent them starting ahead back down the beach to their trucks. Then he took Marissa's chin in his cupped hand and lifted her face to his, staring her in the eyes for a moment that lasted forever, made her heart stop beating in her chest and her breath halt in her lungs. At first she thought he might kiss her—hoped, in fact, and felt her lips part slightly with anticipation. But he only stared, looking deep into her eyes as though she held some sort of answers there.

Then he dropped her chin and looked away, stepping off the low rocks and moving without a moment's hesitation in the direction of his guards, not even waiting to see if she'd follow.

THAT NIGHT, after they'd made their long journey home and the palace was by and large asleep, he went to her. He hadn't meant to. He certainly hadn't planned it. But after lying in bed for an hour, tossing and turning and thinking of nothing but the way the sun had glinted off her profile while she'd looked out at the sea and let the wind play in the loose strands of hair around her neck, he gave up. He wanted her tonight, more than he'd ever wanted anything in his life. And she was lying only one long hallway away. Without a second thought, he grabbed the light cotton robe he kept draped over a chair and pulled on a pair of white pajama pants, tightening the drawstring around his waist. He was sure he looked disheveled, but he didn't care. He figured she wouldn't care either.

She didn't. He pounded on her balcony door and she opened it in moments, as if she had been pacing nearby, and when she saw him she didn't look at all surprised—more like relieved. She was dressed in a silky long gown that clung to her breasts and pushed him over the edge. He groaned and slipped into the bedroom, reaching for her as he did, pulling her to him the moment the door was closed behind them. He pinned her against the door as he took her mouth with his. "I need you," he managed to moan between kisses.

"Yes," was all she said.

To his ears, that yes meant a thousand things. *Yes, you need me. Yes, I need you too. Yes, we have to do this.*

Yes, I'm yours, if only for tonight.

He moaned again as she pressed her body into his, and then he took her hand and led her to the bed, tossed her on top of it and began to slide his hands up and under her gown. She trembled at his touch and closed her eyes in ecstasy. "Yes," she said again, as at last he took exactly what he needed.

10

THOUGH THEY NEVER DISCUSSED WHAT WAS HAPPENING, THEY PASSED a week this way, Khalid attending to his business all day, then coming to her at night by way of the balcony door. Marissa found herself living for the sound of his knock, praying that he would be there, and every night he was. They made love, unforgettable, unbelievable love that had her mindless with pleasure, and afterward he didn't rush off as she expected him to. He stayed, propped up on his side, and ran his fingers through her hair until she fell asleep or until they were ready for more. Some nights they would stay up late, alternately talking and making love, one leading to the other as smoothly and seamlessly as if they'd been together every day for the last three years, instead of living on different continents. Despite her constant efforts to protect her heart, to remind herself of the facts of her situation, nothing worked, and Marissa found herself falling deeper and deeper into the illusion that he could be hers again. That what they once shared could come back, only deeper and stronger with the years.

And then her period came. It arrived in the morning, thirteen days after their night in Cairo. She'd had a feeling, noticed the telltale emotions that had her hiding in her bedroom the day before and the slight twinge of early cramps, but had ignored them both, telling herself it could be a sign of either outcome. When he came to her room, she'd said nothing of her mood swings, waiting anxiously for real physical evidence. And dreading it at the same time.

That night the sex had been different. Slower than usual, more deliberate. That thick, foreign word he'd used that fateful night in Cairo slipped from his tongue for the first time since. "Marissa. _Habibti,_" he'd whispered as he buried his face in her neck, just before the orgasm vibrated through her body into his. Only now she knew what it meant. She'd looked it up online. It meant _My Love._

Afterward she'd wept, though she'd tried not to let him see. She didn't want to tell him that she suspected hormones were rushing through her in that old familiar way, making her an emotional land mine waiting to go off. But he noticed, rolled over and cupped her body with his own, slid his large hand up her body, and brushed away the tears. He hadn't asked why she was crying. He'd just pushed away her hair and pressed a kiss to the back of her neck and squeezed her tighter. And then he'd fallen asleep that way, his hot breath tickling her back as she tried to quiet her mind and ignore the overpowering sensation of safety she felt in his arms.

When, late the next morning, she saw that she couldn't ignore the evidence anymore, she felt bereaved.

It made no sense. She had come to Cairo for a business trip. She'd had dinner with Khalid for the sake of closure. And she'd gotten it when she'd discovered he'd let gossip ruin their relationship and send him into a fake marriage while she was mourning the death of their child. She hadn't wanted to bear him children. She hadn't wanted to get pregnant at all. She'd spent nights praying it was a false alarm so she could return to her family and go back to the life she'd had before.

Only now she didn't want that life anymore. Now she wanted

a life with Khalid, in his arms, no matter where he was. She wanted to give him the family he'd always longed for. She wanted him to love her the way she knew she loved him.

She knew now that it was something she could never have. Not anymore.

She steeled herself, ignoring the temptation not to tell him, reminding herself that she owed him total honesty in these matters after the way she'd kept him in the dark before. Not telling him about the first pregnancy had been a terrible mistake, and she would not make that mistake again.

She returned to the bedroom and found him there, sitting up in bed, looking hungrily in her direction. She smiled weakly. He swung his legs to the side, rose from the bed, and came to her where she stood.

"It's still early," he growled as he wrapped his arms around her, the desire in him obvious through his thin cotton pants. "Come back to bed with me, send me off into the day properly."

"Khalid," she started, stepping backwards out of his arms. This was impossible when he stood so close. His touch made it impossible to think. "It came."

He looked at her, confused, for a long time, his arms still extended so he could hold her. Then she saw the comprehension dawn on his face, felt as he dropped his hands to his sides, turned his face to the floor. "I see," he said at last. His face was unreadable from this angle. What was he feeling? Relieved? Dejected? Some mix of both?

"So I guess it was a false alarm after all," she said, fighting to keep the disappointment out of her voice. She pushed her lips into a false smile. "We were worried over nothing."

"Right," he replied, and for a second, she thought maybe he too was disappointed. He looked back up, shoved the fall of hair that had tumbled into his eyes out of the way. "It's just that, I thought last night, when you were crying, that maybe that was hormones, making you emotional." Her heart tugged against itself when she remembered the closeness she'd felt to him just eight hours ago. "I didn't realize it was the other kind of hormones." His voice sounded dejected. Could he have wanted the same thing as she? Then he shattered the illusion. "Well," he said, shrugging his shoulders as though he'd just run a marathon. "What a relief, right?"

She nodded, unable to trust her voice.

"I guess we dodged a bullet," he went on, never looking her in the eye. He walked to the point on the floor where she'd pushed him out of his robe the night before and grabbed it up, slid his arms into it, and belted it around his narrow waist. "Now life can return to normal." He made "normal" sound like a good thing, when it was the last thing in the world she wanted.

"Yes," she said weakly. "Normal. Khalid?" She had no idea what she wanted to say to him. Could she tell him that she wanted to stay here, with him, even though there was no reason to? It was ridiculous, and he would laugh at her. She floundered around desperately searching for some excuse to stay, but came up empty.

"Yes?" he asked, and already that old impatience was back in his voice.

"Nothing," she said at last, feeling like a fool. Telling him how she was feeling was the stupidest thing she could do. He'd known exactly how much she loved him before, and that hadn't stopped him from breaking her heart. "Sorry, I'm just so relieved I can hardly think," she added, deciding that at this point she was entitled to a small lie to protect her dignity. "It's just such a load off my mind."

At those words, he did look at her again, but the softness of his expression was gone, replaced by irritation. He raised his eyebrows slightly, set his jaw in a scowl. "I'm sure it is."

There was no doubt—their affair was officially over. He couldn't wait to see the back of her.

"Very well. Later you can meet up with Jana to arrange your

travel. I'm sure we can have you back home in a matter of days. Maybe sooner." She wished he didn't sound so ready to be rid of her. "So. I'll see you at dinner tonight," he said darkly as he moved toward the balcony door. "Maybe we should have a celebration."

"Mmm," she replied, anxious for him to get out, so he wouldn't see her cry at the thought of celebrating this outcome. "Have a nice day," she called after him lamely as he slipped out the way he had come, and the door closed with a click behind him.

A nice day? He was already planning his celebration. Which would involve, no doubt, anyone but her. Whereas she knew exactly where she would be today. Crumpled up on the floor alone. Wondering how she'd let herself get hurt by him all over again.

THE MOMENT he was safely on the balcony, alone, Khalid let his pinched face fall into a frown, his hands tighten into angry fists. A false alarm, she'd called it. A load off her mind.

How nice for her. Now she could go back to her American life, the life she'd been so ready to raise his son alone in the first time around. A life without him.

But she'd seemed so different over the last week. Ever since they'd visited the northern beach, she'd talked as though she'd wanted to be here, almost as though she hoped she were pregnant.

He was an idiot to believe her interest in him or Rifaisa could last. The only reason she was willing to stay here was because he was making her. How many times did he have to learn that lesson before he'd stop wanting her, stop thinking about her body and her hands and her eyes every goddamned second of the day?

With a muffled groan he stormed back to his bedroom. There

was no point in standing here mooning around about a child—hell, about a family—that wasn't meant to be.

When he opened the door he heard the telltale sound of his mobile phone chirping. It was Amid, and he ignored the call, not trusting himself not to yell bloody murder at the first poor soul he ran up against this morning. But when the caller gave up, he looked at his emails and saw repeated missives from Jana and Amid. He clicked through them. The contract he'd nailed down in Cairo was in danger of falling through. Someone, a dark horse, had come in with a lowball offer. There was a good chance the whole agreement could fall apart before the day was out.

Good, thought Khalid. He knew it was selfish, but he needed an emergency to distract him. He couldn't just sit around all day waiting for the disappointment to wash over him like a tide going out to sea. He quickly typed back to both aides that they needed to arrange a quick flight to the home of the sheikhs he'd been dealing with. Jana would attend, he decided. The last thing he needed was one of Amid's indiscreet side comments about Marissa at a time like this.

Then, as an afterthought, he added a separate email just to Jana, telling her that Marissa would need assistance in planning her return to the States, and that if she wanted to wait for his business to conclude, she could use the private jet for her trip—it was up to her. Explaining no further, he hit send, clicked off his mobile, and made for the shower. *There*, he thought with satisfaction. He'd offered Marissa an easy way out. He'd be away for at least a couple of days. She could take a commercial flight and never even have to say good-bye. Or, if she chose to wait, well, then that would mean that maybe they had a second chance.

She wouldn't wait, he reminded himself. She'd made no secret that she was anxious to be out from under him. Though she'd seemed so comfortable in that position, he remembered with an anguished grimace. Again he thanked his luck that he had a reason to get out of Rifaisa for enough time to forget the amazing sex they'd shared. Otherwise, he wasn't sure he'd *let* her leave. And more time together was the last thing either of them needed.

As he packed his bags and pulled on the traditional robes and lightweight wool trousers that were appropriate for his destination, he reminded himself that there would be other women. If it was a child he wanted so much—and judging from the intense disappointment he was battling, he did—there would be a line of women just waiting to become princesses upon his return. Women who would be more docile and more trustworthy.

Women who paled in comparison to Marissa.

But that was how life was, he knew. Full of compromises. He was, by now, used to giving up things he wanted—his old life, his freedom, his privacy—to be a dutiful leader. And even before, when he'd been a boy, he'd given up dreams of family before he'd been old enough to understand the word "compromise." Now he would give up Marissa—and whatever it was about her that he found so hard to resist—to marry someone more reliable—to make sure his children never had to feel that loss that had followed him around his entire life.

It was the right thing to do. The only thing to do.

Khalid looked down. Somehow he'd managed to stuff a suitcase full of clothes and ready himself for his trip without being able to think straight. He hoped he hadn't just packed six pairs of pants and nothing else, he thought wryly. But if he had, he was the prince of Rifaisa. Someone would give him a pair of shoes and never say a word about what on earth he was thinking, who was distracting him so much this morning. Hell, they probably wouldn't even realize he packed his own bags.

And the only woman who would dare to point out his shortcomings would be on a plane, bound for the States and out of his life for good.

Which was exactly how he wanted it.

Marissa was in the pool when she discovered Khalid was gone. She'd spent an hour wallowing in her bedroom before she'd reared up and decided she couldn't just lie around all day. Every day since they'd arrived she'd gone for a swim in the beautiful glassed-in pool off the north side of the palace, and it had helped her work off her nervous energy while waiting for an answer. Today she hoped it would help distract her from the sharp ache in her chest that came from knowing for sure she wasn't pregnant and wishing for something she should never have wanted.

She pulled on the modest teal blue one-piece that Jana had found for her and slipped into the warm water, letting herself imagine that, like a load of dirty laundry, all she needed was a good soak. It did help—for as long as she kept moving her arms through the water. The moment she stopped, exhausted and breathing hard from the work of kicking her legs, it all came rushing back—her period, seeing the look on Khalid's face this morning, and watching him walk away.

And then she noticed she was not alone. A maid she recognized was standing by the side of the water, watching her intently. She swam to the edge and hung off the side of the pool. "Good morning," she said in Arabic. It was the only phrase she'd really mastered so far. Well, that and "Good evening." She had always had such a tough time with languages.

The woman smiled politely and nodded her head slightly. Then she began to speak in a very wary English that Marissa appreciated enormously. "Amid sends me," she began, and then paused a long time to find more words. "I tell you," she went on, "the prince is leave. You come with me?" Marissa noticed she held an enormous fluffy white robe, and pulled herself out of the water, her heart sinking.

Of course the prince is leave, she thought. *He is leave at the first chance he gets.*

She toweled off and wrapped herself in the long heavy robe, letting the maid fuss with the neckline until not an inch of skin remained visible. Then she slipped her feet into the closed-toed slippers she'd brought with her and followed her obediently, knowing Amid was waiting with her marching orders, too modest to step inside the pool room while she was in swimwear. When she found him waiting in the great hall, he stood politely and smiled the biggest smile she'd seen on his face since she'd met him.

"Ms. Madden," he said smoothly, dismissing the maid with a tip of the head. "My apologies for interrupting your swim. The prince said you would want to leave as soon as possible and I wanted to help you plan your travel." He paused. "Was the other swimming suit not to your liking?"

"The other?"

"From the yacht."

Amid had given her that bikini? Suddenly the reek of chlorine lingering on her skin made her nauseated. She wanted to rush away and hide in the shower and avoid this conversation. She wanted to avoid the humiliation of being dismissed by Khalid's staff. Instead she dug deep and forced her biggest smile back at him. "Thank you, Amid. How very thoughtful of you."

His own smile faltered as he gestured to a pair of armchairs nearby and they both sat down. "Mr. Abbasi had to leave quite suddenly on business, so he sends his apologies. He wishes to provide you the best-quality travel back to Cairo, where I can arrange with your airline to schedule the deferred ticket to Las Vegas."

"I'd appreciate that."

"The earliest flight to Cairo leaves tonight, meaning you'll need to spend the night there and fly to the States tomorrow, assuming I can secure tickets in time. Would you like a room in the Four Seasons again, or would you prefer different accommodations?"

"The Four Seasons is more than fine, thank you," she replied, but then thought again. "It's really no emergency. I'm happy to stay here tonight, rather than spend the night in a hotel."

Amid's face twisted slightly, adding to Marissa's suspicions. "Certainly. In that case I'll arrange travel for first thing tomorrow morning, with a connecting flight in the afternoon." He looked at his watch and paused for only a moment. "You'll be back in Las Vegas by midnight local time."

Marissa raised her eyebrows, impressed by Amid's mental calculations of flight durations and time zones. Clearly it was his sharp mind that had taken him so far in his career, since his manners left something to be desired. "That sounds fine," she said. "Will the prince be back by this evening from his business?" *Would she get to say good-bye?*

"Most likely not," Amid replied, shaking his head pleasantly. "I'll just be off to arrange the tickets now," he said, starting to rise.

"Wait." Forgetting herself, Marissa caught him by the arm to hold him back in the seat. He practically jumped to get away from her touch, and at once she remembered how Jana had reminded her not to touch men in public, unless she felt very sure they wouldn't mind. Pulling her hand back, she apologized, first in Arabic, then in English. "I'm so sorry—I forgot." She put her hands pointedly in her lap, watching Amid's eyes as they followed her movement. "I just wanted to ask you if it would be possible to delay my trip home, just until the prince returned?"

Amid practically sneered at her at her request. Marissa frowned. Was she really being that much trouble? "I suppose that could be arranged," he said, not disguising his irritation. "The prince *did* offer you the use of his private jet should you care to wait for his return to the palace."

Marissa thought this over for a moment. Something about the way that last statement was phrased, she wondered if it would be unwise to accept. But she wanted, so badly, to see him one more time. She wanted to say good-bye properly, not vanish into the ether as he had done.

And there was no point in denying it. She wanted to give him one more chance. Not that she thought he would take it. But it couldn't stop her from hoping.

"That would be perfect," she said brightly, ignoring the annoyance that Amid made no effort to disguise.

"I'm not sure that is what the prince prefers," he said, and the words gave Marissa so much doubt she almost changed her mind back to the previous option to cut and run without ever seeing Khalid again.

Then she thought about how she'd felt when he'd done that to her—disappeared out of her life bit by bit and never formally said good-bye. She decided she could not, no matter how much it hurt, do that to someone she loved.

And she knew she loved Khalid.

She knew something in his heart was keeping him from loving her back, despite everything they'd shared, despite the way they could still talk to each other as best friends and make love as soulmates. But knew too, that what she felt for him was nothing less than the real thing, whether it was requited or not.

"I'm sure he'll understand," Marissa said, not sure of any such thing but refusing to let Amid bully her. "So it's settled. I'll stay here until he comes back from his business. Then we'll organize my travel home." Without waiting for another annoyed look or disapproving comment from Amid, she stood and smiled at him brightly and strode out of the hall with her head held high.

BUT WHEN KHALID did not return the next day, or the day after, Marissa began to doubt her decision. Was he purposely staying away so he wouldn't have to see her again? Every day Amid came to her and suggested she consider booking her travel, and every day she politely turned him down. But by the fourth day, she began to waver. Desperate for a confidante, she decided to break her silence with the outside world and talk to someone who could help her understand what was going on. Thank goodness for videochat.

When she got Grant and Jenna on the line, she instantly felt better. Something about seeing her friends, who'd had their own rocky time with love, gave her so much more strength.

"Why did I let myself get so isolated?" she asked them, after catching them up just enough.

"We'd like to know the same thing," Grant exclaimed. "It says here your last log-on was two weeks ago—the last time we talked. And then we get that voicemail from you saying you've decided to stay in Cairo." He shook his head.

"What this control-freak is trying to say is, how can you do this to us?" Jenna reached out to the screen as if she could strangle Marissa over the Internet. "I had Knox on the phone so fast after I got that voicemail, and he calmed me down, but still."

"I'm sorry, guys," Marissa said, clasping her hands together as if begging for forgiveness. "Things happened so fast. After I talked to my brother I just figured he'd keep you in the loop."

"Lucky for you, he did," said Jenna, her voice teasing. "So what's the deal? You're in love with Khalid and never coming back?"

"Hardly," Marissa answered defensively. Then she corrected herself. "Hardly about the never coming back part, at least."

"But the love part?"

Thanking the technology that allowed her not to answer aloud, she nodded her head yes. "I'm not sure how it happened."

Both of her friends looked at her, shocked. "But Marissa," Jenna whined, "he left you all alone last time. Deserted you and married another woman."

"It turns out there's more to that story than we realized. He believed some tabloid gossip and let his imagination run wild."

"That's idiotic," said Grant.

"As idiotic as when you thought I was trying to steal your company?" asked Jenna pointedly.

Grant frowned at this reference to his past romantic foibles. "That was dumb. But this is dumber."

"Maybe," said Marissa, "but so was my letting him slip away. For all the dumb mistakes he made, I made one just as large: I didn't fight for him. Because it was easier to just let him go than to relive the pain I felt about losing his baby. And now for all I know he's gone for good and doesn't plan to come back to his own palace until he's gotten word I've left. Or maybe he'll come back with the wife he really wants. Someone more suitable to marry a prince."

Jenna growled at that, and Marissa couldn't stop a smile at her friend's protectiveness. "You are perfectly suitable. He should be so lucky to be married to a wonderful person like you."

"Thanks," she said, letting her friend's kind words wash over her. "But at the same time, I can see where our relationship would be tricky for his citizens to swallow. He has so many responsibilities to juggle. On top of which, he doesn't think he can trust me."

Grant leaned into the screen. "Is there any reason you can think of that would lead him to distrust you?"

Marissa rolled her eyes. "Are you being sarcastic?"

Confused, he furrowed his brow and shook his head. "No, of course not. What do you mean by that?"

"I mean of course he wouldn't trust me. I never told him about the baby I lost. Even before the accident. And given Khalid's history in the foster system after being dumped by his own father, that's enough to feel totally betrayed."

Grant's mouth popped open in a round O shape. "Okay, I get why you'd think that would make him distrustful, but you explained why you didn't tell him, right? He has to understand the circumstances by now."

Marissa nodded. "I tried, but it didn't seem to make much difference. He's really upset about it."

Jenna tilted her head. "Well, from where I sit, if he has a forgiving bone in his body, he should have seen fit by now to see that situation from your side and let it go. After all, if he had come back for you like he'd promised, you'd have never kept the pregnancy a secret."

Marissa chewed on her friend's words. "Stupid tabloids."

"Let me tell you about my own experiences with successful men," Jenna said, nodding her head toward Grant. "Sometimes they're too stubborn to realize how much they love you, so they push you away just to protect themselves. But they have to work that out for themselves. And if they don't, another guy is just around the corner."

Marissa nodded again, but inside she couldn't have disagreed more. Khalid was a fine man. He had done great things for his country, and for the natural world around him. He gave up so much to do his duty. And she knew for sure no one could ever make her feel as amazing as he had in just a few short weeks.

"What are you thinking right now, Mari?" asked Jenna. "You've got that faraway look in your eye."

Caught out in her thoughts, Marissa confessed. "I'm thinking that you are partly right. There probably is something on his mind that's keeping him from trusting me all the way, and until I know what that is, I'm staying here. I'm not letting this slip away again over a stupid misunderstanding. If this isn't going to work, fine. But before I leave with my tail between my legs, I'm going to be honest about how I feel and make sure it's really over."

Jenna shook her head adamantly. "You can't do that. You'll end up getting your heart broken. Please come home," she begged. But then her husband held up one hand, and she looked at him, her words halting.

"If she wants to take this chance, she should," he said. "Remember this: Marissa was the one who talked you into giving me that second chance. She was right then. Maybe she's doing the right thing now." He turned to face the screen. "Do what's in your heart. But if it doesn't work out—"

"—and we're just a bit worried that it won't," interrupted Jenna.

"If it doesn't work out, we're here for you." Grant finished.

"We love you, Marissa," added Jenna. "Keep us updated. If you need someone to talk to while you're waiting for him to come back, just call."

"Thanks, guys. Believe me, I will. And I love you too," she said, and they disconnected. Marissa leaned back from her laptop, let herself flop over on the bed where Khalid had shown her so much, had reawakened a part of her that she'd forgotten could still exist. The passionate part. She would be damned if she let that go so easily. The last time he'd left, she'd just let him go without a fight. And then, after she'd lost the baby, she'd avoided his calls for months, so absorbed in her own grief that she couldn't even think of what he must have been feeling. This time she'd do whatever it took to see things through his eyes. And if that didn't work—and she was so, so afraid that it wouldn't—at least she'd know she'd tried.

It didn't matter if it took him months to come back. She would wait. As long as it took.

11

KHALID WAS A LONG WAY FROM HIS PALACE. BUT HE FOUND SOON enough that everything reminded him of his home and the woman he'd left there. The woman who was no doubt gone by now. It was day five on his interminable business trip, and still he had no contract nailed down, and no rest from the constant thoughts of Marissa that chased him into every business meeting and legal wrangling session. He thanked the heavens he was able to bring Jana along for this trip—she was so easily able to cover for his mental wanderings that he hardly needed to be there except as a figurehead.

Now she was holding court with a room full of men in their *thawbs*, long, lightweight white robes that matched Khalid's exactly, except in the detailing of the white-on-white embroidery that embellished their plackets. In her own professional-looking *abaya*, with her young assistant dressed similarly poised next to her taking minutes, Jana seemed every bit the part of the high-ranking royal aide, regardless of her gender. In fact, Khalid thought, she was a much more appropriate companion for a crown prince than Marissa could ever be. If he were smart, he'd find a woman like Jana to become his wife. Someone who knew his country well already, who could speak the language and navigate the conventions of the Arabian Peninsula without hesitation.

Only now that Marissa was back in his life, that wasn't what he wanted anymore.

After the meeting was over and the conference room had cleared out, Khalid lingered, pretending to be checking his phone for messages, even though he'd have noticed if it had vibrated in the last half hour. Which it hadn't. He opened and reread the email he'd gotten from Amid for the third time that day. The email that had told him, apologetically, that Marissa remained at the palace, determined to wait for the use of his jet. By now Khalid could have sent it back and forth three times while he worked in Kuwait City, but he did no such thing, against his better judgment. Despite every self-protective bone in his body, he wanted her to be there when he returned. He wanted to get the chance to say good-bye properly.

Hell, he wouldn't mind a chance at a *very* intimate farewell.

That, he told himself, was why he hadn't sent her away just yet. One last horizontal goodbye was all he needed to get her out of his system. Then he'd be ready to let her go and get down to the business of producing an heir with a more appropriate partner.

But he knew he was lying to himself. He knew one more night with Marissa wouldn't be enough. A thousand more nights with her wouldn't be enough. And he would just have to live with that.

"Mr. Abbasi?" Jana poked her head back into the conference room.

"Sorry, Jana," he said, rising up in his seat and making his way toward the exit. "I was just checking on an issue back at the palace." Quite an issue, he thought. One without any satisfactory solution.

"Of course," she said. "Whenever you're ready, our car is waiting to take us back to the hotel for the night."

Surprised, Khalid consulted his watch. Sure enough, it was pushing six p.m. The day had passed before him in a blur of meetings, and he'd hardly even noticed. He sighed, knowing they were nowhere near settling this matter. Another day would pass with her in the palace and him here wondering how much longer she planned on sticking around. Already he'd been surprised at her patience. Now he was beginning to think—okay, *hope*—that she was waiting for him. Why else would she still be there?

He and Jana made their way down to the street level where a black SUV waited on their arrival. Once their party—Jana, her assistant, and a couple of the poor bodyguards he found so damn irritating—had climbed into the vehicle, they began their trip back to the hotel yet again. Khalid felt the surge of grouchiness begin to set in. He told himself it was from the damned monotony of this business trip and the complete lack of progress they were making.

But in reality he knew it was because he wanted to get back to *her*.

Without meaning to, he growled to himself in frustration.

Sitting next to him in the middle row of seats, Jana leaned her head in toward him. "Sir?"

"Sorry, Jana," he said immediately, wishing for the fortieth time that he could be alone with his thoughts for a moment.

"I have meant to tell you," she said quietly enough for no one else to take notice. "That our guest plans to stay at the palace again tonight."

"So I heard from Amid," he replied, matching his volume to hers.

"I wonder if you wouldn't mind my contacting Ms. Madden to make sure she has everything she needs. She might be more comfortable making requests of me, since we've had a chance to speak more often than she and Amid have."

Khalid scrutinized Jana's face, wondering what his aide was hinting at. Jana was not one for gossip, he knew. He watched as she smiled openly, and then she twirled her wedding band absentmindedly. Maybe she wasn't a gossip, but she certainly was a romantic.

"That's unnecessary," Khalid replied simply. "I'm sure Amid is handling things capably back at the palace," he added. As Khalid had let Amid know in his reply email, Amid was to inform Marissa just how long she could be waiting. And if she was still there when he returned, then, and only then, he would hope.

THREE DAYS LATER, with a completely secured deal under his belt at last, Khalid walked into the palace with undisguised anticipation over seeing Marissa. He knew from Jana's now daily reports that she was still here, and that she wanted to see him upon his return. The time he'd spent away from her had opened his eyes to just how disappointed he was at not yet becoming a father, and how dishonest he'd been with Marissa when he'd kept that from her. Perhaps she'd felt the same way, but he'd never given her the chance to say so.

And yes, the trip had given him time to miss her. And miss her he had. He was beginning to believe that he could trust her again, and that it would be worth it to do so. She could be the woman he'd wanted her to be three years ago. The two of them might still have a chance.

He heard his own determined footsteps across the marble-tiled entryway as he strode toward his offices to deposit the briefcase that had felt chained to his wrist over the last week, and then he halted for a moment. Where in the palace would he find her at four p.m.? Swimming? Or in the library, perhaps? Jana had told him she'd taken a series of tours around the city, and he hoped like hell she wasn't off on some sightseeing trip now. He had been waiting a week to find out why she wasn't returning home. He could hardly wait another minute.

He started for the pool, and when he found it empty, reversed his path and headed down the long, narrow corridor to the curved stairs that led up to the library. Just as he reached the first step, he saw a figure rushing toward him in the corner of his eye. Was it her? he wondered briefly—only to see it was just Amid, practically scampering to him, hollering, "Sir, sir!"

Annoyed to be delayed for even another minute, Khalid sighed and stepped back down to the floor, leaning against the railing with his arms crossed impatiently. "Hello, Amid."

"Nice to see you back, sir," his aide panted. "I'm sorry to interrupt, but there's a sensitive matter I feel I must discuss with you. It's really very urgent."

Concerned by Amid's flustered demeanor, his mind suddenly racing with a flurry of potential catastrophes, Khalid uncrossed his arms and led him down to a quiet alcove a few feet away. "What is it?"

His aide's voice was hushed. "It's your guest, sir. Ms. Madden."

Khalid's heart began to pound. "What about her? Is she sick? Has she gotten hurt somehow?"

"Oh, no, she seems to be quite well."

Khalid sent a silent prayer of thanks at that, and began to coax his breathing back to normal. Amid must never gave him a scare like that again.

"But—and I hope you don't find this impertinent," Amid went on, "I felt it vital that I report to you on her unusual behavior while you were absent."

"Unusual behavior?" Khalid parroted, then remembered himself. "I don't care in the least about her behavior," he added, attempting to keep his face neutral rather than confirm all the gossip about the nature of their relationship.

"If I may speak frankly," Amid said, lowering his voice so much that Khalid had to lean in to hear him. "I try not to listen to gossip, but the idle talk of palace maids has led me to believe you are engaged in some sort of relationship with Ms. Madden."

Khalid's blood boiled at that. "If that were true, it certainly wouldn't fall under the purview of your office."

"Perhaps," Amid persisted, holding up a single finger as if to beg for a moment to explain. "But one of my jobs as your chief aide is seeing that everyone who enters this palace is of worthy character. And Ms. Madden, in my judgment, is most unworthy."

Khalid felt his face harden into a cold glare. "You had better explain that statement quickly," he said, his voice menacing. He'd known from the start that his staff would gossip about Marissa or any woman he spoke to more than once, but now he had been pushed too far. He had quite enough of all this speculation.

"Every night since you've left," Amid went on, undaunted, "she's been on her personal computer, talking to an American man in her bedroom, late into the evening. Perhaps she doesn't realize how closely we monitor the Internet usage here in the palace. It is obvious that their relationship is quite intimate, considering the manner in which they converse."

Khalid realized he had to unclench his teeth to speak. "How so?"

"The English phrase 'I love you' seems a clear enough indication," Amid said, eyes fixed on Khalid's. "His name is Grant, or so I've gathered from their conversations, though I haven't been able to determine a last name yet."

Grant. Blakely. The very same man she'd been in the car accident with. On their way to pick out an engagement ring—apparently for Grant's wife, Jenna. Seething, Khalid rose to his full height, towering over his aide, and fought the urge to break the first thing he saw. His muscles were so tense, he found, he was nearly shaking with fury. But could Marissa have been lying this whole time? Grant was married, Khalid had had that information confirmed. But Grant's marriage didn't mean that he didn't have a mistress on the side. Marissa.

She'd been waiting in his palace for days, making him think she was pining for him, when every night she'd been cooing to a man back home. Unable to control himself, he picked up a fragile-looking object in the palm of his hand and then dashed it down to the marble floor in an explosion of shards and noise. "Damn her!" he shouted, annoyed at his own inability to control his emotions. Struggling for control, he looked to Amid and found him still sitting, hands folded in his lap as though he was proud of his spy work. At once, Khalid couldn't stand to be in his presence.

"We don't spy on our guests in this palace," he said through his hard-set jaw, though he felt the hypocrisy of his words even before they were spoken. He had to get out of here. He needed just one goddamned minute alone to deal with this bit of news. "I'll discuss that issue with you later," he muttered, as he fled the scene, his shoes crunching over the shattered bit of china that he hoped wasn't too much of a priceless family heirloom.

Though frankly, he was too furious to care much either way. He had made a fool of himself—not just now, in front of Amid, but in front of everyone who watched him, and it seemed these days that that was everyone he met. *Of course* they had whispered about his nighttime visits to her, *of course* they had noticed his every move. They'd known what he was doing better than he had. For what he'd been doing was lunacy.

And now he saw just what an idiot he'd been. For he'd let himself trust the least trustworthy woman he'd ever met. And not just trust her. He'd let himself fall.

MARISSA WAS on her little stretch of balcony wrapped up in a book when Khalid came bursting into her suite, scaring the paperback out of her hands onto the cool tile floor. She stood up at once, looking from him to the door of her chamber, through which he'd come, realizing that he'd just tramped through her bedroom and probably seen the mess of clothes that came from packing and unpacking her bags at least once daily. But what did she care? He was back, and the moment she laid eyes on him she broke into a silly grin, so happy to see his face again, even if he was scowling at her. Well, she hadn't expected him to be happy about her waiting for his return, she reminded herself. She would have to convince him that it had been for a good reason. And it had been.

"Khalid," she whispered, as though they'd been apart for a year, not a week. Unable to control herself she went to him and put her arms around him, pressed her face into his strong chest and inhaled deeply. Feeling his body so stiff in her arms, she pulled back sheepishly. He was angry. She had a lot of explaining to do.

"Listen, Khalid," she said, still standing an arm's length from him, looking up into his hard eyes for any trace of feeling and finding none. "I'm sorry I'm still here," she said. "I know you wanted me to leave. I know it seems like there's no reason for me to stay."

Not saying a word, he nodded his head just an inch. Marissa's heart began to pound. "After we found out I wasn't pregnant, there was nothing keeping me here. I should have wanted to get on the next plane for Vegas. After all, you had forced me into coming here in the first place. But the thing is, I didn't want to leave."

Still his face remained impassive. She told herself it was now or never. And as safe as *never* sounded, she owed it to herself to go for it now. "I didn't want to leave because," she pressed her lips together as if trying to hold back the words, but then she forced them out. "Because I've fallen in love with you all over again." She paused, looked up at him waiting, hoping he would say something back.

But the ice in his eyes didn't melt at all. Instead he quirked his mouth and lowered his gaze so it seemed to bore a hole in her forehead. "You've fallen in love with me?" he asked, his voice distanced and almost amused. "What happened to wanting to be back home with your *loved ones*?"

Marissa swallowed hard. Why was he making this so hard on her? She hadn't expected a tearful exchange of I-love-yous, it was true, but he just seemed to be getting angrier with every word she said.

She wanted to chicken out and run more than ever, but she refused to give up. "I still miss them, but I am beginning to believe there's a way to make this work." She saw him frown even more deeply at that and turned her face away, focused on the floor and began to talk fast, afraid of a moment's silence, terrified of his reaction. "I think Rifaisa is a magical country, and I'm fascinated by its history. I know I could be happy here if we were together. And the thing is, I was, as crazy as it is, I was starting to hope to build a family with you."

With those words out of her mouth, there was no going back now. She locked her eyes with his and pressed on. "I was so hurt, for years, by the way you just disappeared after you came here. I didn't understand why you would abandon me and get married so soon after we stopped talking. But that's in part because I didn't see what you were going through on your end. I'm beginning to understand a lot better how much pressure you're under in your new life, and how distanced it can feel from the rest of the world in this palace."

Khalid's face fixed into a grimace. She didn't dare look him in the eye as she pushed on. "And I know I didn't make things easy back then, the way I kept my pregnancy a secret from you and then holed up and wouldn't talk to you after the accident. I know you're still angry about that, and I understand that, but I was dying of grief, Khalid. I'd never gone through anything so painful before." She closed her eyes to ward off the memory of it and swallowed hard.

"But I think enough time has passed, and I've proven that I can be trusted and it's time to forgive me. So I guess, what I'm trying to say is, I stayed here, even after you were gone, even after you sent Amid to schedule my departure over and over, because I wanted to ask you if you thought you had it in you to let the past go."

At the mention of Amid trying to schedule her departure, Khalid looked at her quizzically, showing, finally, a break in his angry demeanor.

"If you're willing to let go, Khalid, I know we can make this thing between us work once and for all. I still want to share my life with you. I want to keep trying for a family—with you. You got me believing I could try for a pregnancy again, and I know there's no one else on earth who could have done that."

Suddenly out of words, she sat down in a heap on the bench, almost unable to believe what she'd just said. Could he believe it? That was all that mattered.

She looked up into his face, saw in his eyes something so far away that for a moment she wondered if he'd heard a word she'd just said. God, she hoped so. She couldn't imagine trying to say it all again.

"Khalid?" she said, when he said nothing in response.

"Yes," he replied, his voice stiff and matter of fact, as if she'd just called a business meeting to order, not declared her love for him.

She was flustered, confused. She'd prepared herself for all kinds of responses from him, but indifference wasn't one of them. "I just poured my heart out to you," she said. "Don't you have anything to say back?" She knew she sounded like a scolding teacher, but she didn't care. Her heart was on a skewer in front of him, and he was ignoring it altogether.

"I do have something to say," he told her. "Get. Out."

Marissa gasped in a breath.

"You have the gall, the nerve, to stand there and tell me you think we can make it work again? That you still love me after all these years? While every night you've been online, chatting with your lover back in America?"

She was stunned. "My *what?*"

"I know everything, Marissa," he said, his voice like daggers. "You actually had me convinced that Grant and Jenna were your friends, that Grant wasn't your lover like I suspected all those years ago."

"That's because he isn't." She couldn't believe what she was hearing. Khalid had lost his mind.

"What was your plan, Marissa? To marry me, and what, use your connections in Rifaisa to create opportunities for your lover's empire?"

She was so horrified by his words that she didn't know whether to defend herself or laugh.

"But here's the damnedest thing, Marissa," he said, pointing a finger at her angrily. "You actually had me going there. I was starting to think that you really wanted to be here with me."

"I do."

He laughed coldly at her words. "I don't believe you. I have proof of your affair."

Marissa knew it was an opportunity, this pause in his diatribe, for her to ask him where he'd gotten his so-called proof, but suddenly she didn't want to. If he thought she was capable of all that he'd said, then what was the point of trying to make him believe otherwise? What was the point of any of this?

"Go on, please," she uttered coolly. "This is fascinating."

"Is it?" he asked. "Are you captivated by the tale of the prince who fell for one of Scheherazade's stories? Let himself believe that she'd changed her ways and was ready to start a family, to be together as they'd been before, only here, in his country, where he belongs? Because the story takes a tragic turn. Our hero leaves town for just one week, and when he comes back, his aides give him a detailed report of the long, loving conversations between his supposed true love and the very same man she left him for in the first place. Every night. Long into the night. I must imagine this Grant misses you very much, Marissa. Did you happen, at any point in these frequent conversations, to mention my name?"

Feeling her heart turn to ice in a way she'd never before experienced, Marissa tilted her head and shot Khalid the hardest smile she could muster. "As a matter of fact, I did," she said. "But now that I see what you think of me, I wish we hadn't wasted so much breath on you." She turned, ready to make her way into the bedroom, throw everything she could fit into a suitcase, and get home any way she could. She'd just told him she loved him and wanted to have his children, and in response he'd accused her of the most ridiculous, utterly imaginary, insulting nonsense she'd ever heard. She'd be happy never to see him again.

"I'll be out of your way now, Khalid," she hissed, about to turn her back on him forever. But just as she did, a tiny voice whispered into her head: *Tell him the truth. Let him see what an idiot he's been, so he knows what he's lost in you.* "But before I go," she said, advancing slightly back on him, trying to ignore the look of fury and indignation on his face, "I'd like to add a few extra details to your little scenario. I did talk to Grant Blakely several times while you were gone."

He snorted derisively.

"Along with his wife, Jenna. They tried to convince me to leave you, that you would hurt me again. I said that I needed to stay and tell you the truth about my love for you. Every call ended the same way. They said, *We love you.* I said, *I love you, too.* Someday, I hope you have such loving friends."

She reached on the floor and picked up a piece of clothing, jamming it into her suitcase. She couldn't even stand to look at him anymore.

"And then, every day, your assistant, Amid, made me feel like you wanted me to leave. That I was in the way. That it was inappropriate for me to be here. But I persevered. I bet it was Amid who told you I was talking to some man at night."

She glanced up at him when she said that, and the shocked look on his face told her she'd guessed right. "He did! You're so gullible. Can't you see he's been pitting you against me?" She jammed more clothes into her suitcase. She was almost packed. "I love you Khalid, but I also love myself. And I deserve someone who is rooting for us to be together—not looking for any excuse for us to be apart."

Khalid stared at her, speechless.

"Honestly. All it took was one lie from Amid for you to think I'd marry you under false pretenses and, what, embezzle state funds? Good-bye, Khalid." She threw her eyes over his body one last time—one long last look—and then strode from the bedroom texting Jana as she left.

It was time to move on. She had her closure. At long last.

12

AT MIDNIGHT, THE PORT OF RIFAISA WAS A VERY DIFFERENT PLACE. The docks themselves were dead and dark, as drained of their life as Khalid was feeling as he walked them. But thirty feet away, the waterfront restaurants spilled over with vivacious people, and from afar, the sight of them laughing and embracing each other merrily as they tumbled out of the establishments, full of good food and friendship, seemed like lemon juice over a wound. He was glad to be shouting distance away from them, and gladder still when he made it to his destination, the royal yacht where he could, he hoped, hide away for at least one night. He hoped one night would be long enough to summon his composure and come to terms with the fact that he was an utter moron.

At the end of the gangway, he saw one of the shipyard guards he liked especially well pacing the deck of the ship and thanked the heavens for small favors. Khalid waved and pushed aside the heavy black hood he'd worn to the port. For a moment the man looked confused; then he snapped into action as he recognized Khalid and extended the gangway out to the docks, deftly landing it right at Khalid's feet. "Sir," the guard called out, but Khalid waved his arms in front of him to shut him up. Quickly jogging onto the ship, he put his finger to his lips in the universal sign of coercion and whispered, "I'm on the lam from my staff," in English.

The guard made a confused face, and Khalid laughed in spite of his dark mood at his own attempt to use American slang in such a situation. "My apologies," he added in Arabic, then explained as best he could that he didn't want any company or attention at the moment. If only there was a word in English or Arabic that summed up what an idiot he was. But truly, his level of regret at the moment was beyond the bounds of language.

He thought through every word she'd said for the tenth time. Her words made sense—more sense than Amid's lies, which he'd eaten up with a spoon.

But she'd been so distant three years ago, and he'd been far too ready to accept that it was because she'd found someone else when he'd seen that tabloid. He knew how often women had been pushed on him since his arrival in Rifaisa, and he couldn't help but think her situation was no different. He was no longer an attractive match for her, considering he lived on the other side of the world, miles from the family she cherished so much. And the nation he ruled was smack-dab in the middle of a part of the world few Americans could begin to understand. Why would Marissa, an independent woman with all kinds of dreams, want to move here and put up with all the drastic changes he'd endured?

Except, maybe she *would* have moved, if he'd given her half a chance. Pacing the deck that stretched around the ship's bow, where he could see nothing but dark sky and darker sea, he remembered how he'd reacted when she'd told him about the baby she'd lost. All he could think about was the pain that she'd caused him by hiding his child from him. But now he could see it from her perspective. And he could see how much grief she would have suffered after the miscarriage. It hurt that she hadn't been able to tell him what she'd been going through back then, but he supposed he deserved to be hurt after the way he'd acted, ready to believe the worst of her.

And then his mind went back, as it had every two minutes over the last two hours, to what she'd told him just before his outburst. She had said she loved him.

She loved him.

Correction: She *had* loved him—before he'd shown her in no uncertain terms that he was a buffoon and a jackass. After that, the love in her eyes had gone out like a snuffed candle, and only fury had remained. And maybe disappointment, too. In all the time he'd known her, he'd never heard her talk to anyone in that cold tone she'd used tonight. Frankly, he hadn't known she was capable of such reproach. Maybe no one had earned it before now. How he hated that he had been the first.

Khalid sagged with exhaustion. Knowing rest was not an option, not while his head raged with every choice he'd made, every chance he'd missed to be with her, he made his way up two sets of stairs and took a seat on the sundeck where a bimini just slightly obstructed the 360-degree views. From here he imagined he could make out the dim lights of the rear side of the palace, set high on a man-made hill above the port, and he imagined she might still be there. Or she might not. He realized that his instruction to Jana to set her up in his jet upon his return still stood and that Marissa would not hesitate now to use it. Maybe she was already making her way to the airport. For a moment, he felt envious. If there were some possible way for him to escape his unhappiness by plane at the moment, he would have been eager to do so. He couldn't stand being alone with the realization of what he'd done.

And there was nothing he could do about it now. He had no excuse to keep her here anymore. For at once he realized that an excuse was all that broken condom had been. A reason to be near her again despite all his mental bargaining and justifications. He had told himself all sorts of stories, but ultimately, hadn't he just wanted another moment with the woman who made him feel so incredibly understood? The woman who, he now realized, he'd failed to understand in return.

Too restless to sit, he stood up and started yet another pacing path around the edge of the deck. What about him had made him so willing to believe the worst in her, made him almost want— though it made no sense—to believe she could abandon him as carelessly as his father and mother had in his own infancy? It was almost as if he was forcing her into doing exactly what he'd always thought she'd do, what he'd always thought *everyone* would do. Leave.

With a start, Khalid noticed he was squeezing the back of a captain's chair as if it were his own neck he were wringing. The urge to pick something up in his clenched hands and throw it to the ground, to take some sort of release in the sight of anything shattering across the deck, was stronger than he could understand. He was always clasping onto things, he saw, as if he expected them to slip through his fingers. He'd grabbed onto Marissa with both hands, and in so doing, he'd squeezed the love out of her heart. Love, that, as she'd pointed out, had never gone away, no matter the distance between them. Until now.

As if trying to startle him out of his dark thoughts, Khalid's phone began to vibrate relentlessly in his pants pocket. He pushed his robe out of the way and answered it without even identifying the caller first, so happy to have any excuse not to follow his emotions down this rabbit hole any further. "Yes?" he barked.

"Sir." Jana's voice cut through the line. "I wanted to let you know, sir, that Ms. Madden is departing for the airport." Jana's voice was quiet and resigned, and Khalid realized at once that she, too, had come to enjoy having Marissa around.

"Very well. See that she has a very comfortable and safe trip home, please." He clicked his phone off, not wanting to risk hearing any more questions buried behind Jana's perfectly polite announcements. There, he thought, was the one perk of being royalty. Permission to hang up on people when one was in a terrible mood and didn't want to hear about how he'd driven the woman he loved as far away as she could go.

But then, that was exactly what he should be listening to, he thought with a start. She was heading for the airport, a destination maybe a half hour from the palace in this light evening traffic. He could make it there in twenty if he left this very second. He could be there, waiting, when she arrived, ready to tell her what she deserved to hear. She'd leave anyway, he knew it as sure as he knew what he had to do. But he would tell her anyway. Tell her he loved her. Let her know, at least, that he always had.

JANA WAS Marissa's driver that night. It was late, and the palace was not as bustling with staff as usual. And when they were ready to leave, Khalid's regular driver was nowhere to be found, though he'd been sitting in front of the palace at the ready just ten minutes earlier. No matter. Marissa was happy to have Jana in the car with her, glad to be able to give the kindest person she'd known in her brief time here a proper good-bye. But the route they were taking to the airport was so circuitous that for a moment she wondered if Jana actually knew the way.

As she waited and waited for them to make what she'd assumed would be an easy journey, she stared out the window at the winding roads and sparse traffic and wondered how her trip to Rifaisa had gone so terribly wrong. It was almost as if it had been preordained to end this way, ever since she'd walked into her apartment that terrible day three years ago and found Khalid's grandfather sitting on her sofa. Or had she set this chain of events into motion when she'd failed to tell her lover about her pregnancy?

No, she realized with a sinking heart. Their lives had been set on this path even earlier, when Khalid had been abandoned for the first time and had come to believe that that was how people treated the ones they loved. If that hadn't been in his mind already, lurking, ready to spring up when least expected, then he'd never have leapt to the conclusions he had. He'd have never believed some trashy tabloid—a magazine that her brothers must have kept from her while she was recovering, bless their protective souls—more than he believed his own judgment or experience. He would never have believed that she'd kept a pregnancy from him to hurt him rather than help him.

But he'd done all of those things. He'd let his own distorted life-view get in the way, and now that the shock of it had worn off, Marissa felt idiotic for not seeing it coming sooner.

Oh, she'd known he was damaged, known he'd always had trouble trusting her. He'd always longed for a family while at the same time not truly believing in the concept. But she'd never truly accepted how deep his wounds went. And as a result, she'd let herself believe he could learn how to trust her—she had believed he already had.

But she'd been wrong. All along he'd been assuming she was someone totally different from who she actually was. He believed she was the kind of woman who could forget a man she loved in a month. Who would steal a man's child from him. Who would marry a man while loving another—at that thought, she snorted.

"Is everything okay, Ms. Madden?" Jana asked.

"Yes, of course." Marissa needed to keep her ruminating silent.

Marissa knew that, despite his idiocy, she would never forget Khalid, even over a lifetime. For despite his failings, despite his darkened opinion of her and everyone else who claimed to care about him, she loved him. She'd loved him before, of course, but what they'd had over the last few weeks was something so much more than that first blush of love they'd had back then. Now she was a grown woman, a woman who knew what it was like to lose something you wanted more than anything in the world and still go on. And he was a man who had the weight of a nation on his shoulders and yet could still take her by the hand and make her believe in second chances.

But third chances? No.

In the distance she saw the unmistakable sight of lit-up runways and pulsing strobes that told her she was about to be gone from his life forever. In a matter of minutes she'd be on a plane—his plane, sure, but without him on it—bound for Cairo, and in about 18 hours she'd be back home, in a taxi, headed for her family, with whom she could once again nurse her wounds and get on with her life. She'd done it once. She just hoped her heart could survive this second blow.

Jana pulled their car up to the front gate. "Sorry for the delay," she said smoothly as she unbuckled her seat belt and slid out of the car. Marissa followed her rushed steps to the private entrance where, she assumed, Khalid's jet awaited, all while trying to take in Rifaisa, a country she'd become so attached to, one last time. In a fog of sadness she passed through the glass doors, Jana speaking quickly in Arabic to everyone they met and then shuttling her to the jetway. It was not until Marissa climbed the stairs to the plane and began to take in the now familiar sight of the beautiful private jet that she realized why Jana had been hurrying her so.

For there, pacing like a pent-up panther, was Khalid, dressed in a dark robe and looking every bit the desert prince he'd become. Even now, after he'd broken her heart for the second time, the sight of him sent shivers racing across her skin. He was walking a hole in the aisle until he saw her, and then he moved quickly to where she stood and grabbed her by the shoulders, saying nothing at all, only locking eyes with her. For a moment she let herself look hard into those eyes, his dark irises like a well she could fall into and never find the bottom of. In his eyes she saw the passion they'd shared, the nights he'd come to her, and then more. That day in the gulf at Dubai, how he'd hypnotized her with a touch, then taken her there, in the water, where she felt weightless and light. Her heart began to thump harder in her chest, and she was glad he wasn't speaking because she wasn't sure she'd have been able to hear him. For a moment she was back there letting the waves and his embrace rock her up and down.

Then she came to her senses, thought of everything he'd said to her just a few hours earlier, and stepped back, out of his reach, crossing her arms in front of her. "What are you doing here?" she asked coldly, surprised that she could fake that much disinterest.

"I came to apologize," he said, his voice gruff, hardly what Marissa thought of as an apologetic tone. "I don't want you to go." He still held her shoulders, though his arms were stretched across the gulf of distance between their bodies.

She tried unsuccessfully to wriggle loose. "I don't think there's anything you can say that will make me stay," she said, using first one hand, and then the other, to physically peel his fingers off of her and escape his touch. She turned away from him, as if she could make him vanish with her mind, but then her curiosity got the better of her and she turned back. "I want to go home, Khalid. Please, let me go."

Khalid looked down, dropping his hands to his side. Then he dropped to one knee. "What if I asked you to marry me?"

Marissa froze. She had not expected him to say that. "What?" she choked out.

"Marry me, Marissa," he said again, while she stared at him shocked. "Move here and become my wife." Somehow it sounded more like a command than a proposal.

Her heartbeat moved into a new sprinting rhythm. "No," she

said as solidly as she could muster. "And let me tell you why. Firstly, I don't appreciate being ordered around. And secondly, I don't want to marry a man who doesn't trust me." She set her hands on her hips, wondering where she'd found the strength to do the right thing, and proud of herself at the same time.

Undaunted, he caught her hand in both of his and held it there. "It's not that I didn't trust you, Marissa," he replied, still down on one knee. "It's that I didn't trust anyone. When I fell in love with you the first time—hell, the only time, because it's not as if I am ever going to get over you—I told myself you were too good to be true. That it was only a matter of time until you were done with me, just like everyone else who'd claimed to love me."

Marissa exhaled loudly, too frustrated and overcome to stay silent. "Khalid, I'm not an idiot. I knew all of this." Except for the love part, she realized. That was news to her. Good news, though she tried not to accept it. "I think I always have known, or at least, ever since you told me about what it was like being passed from foster home to foster home, always knowing that your family would be temporary. I knew you would have trouble trusting me. I just thought you'd be able to learn how over time." She frowned and looked down to him where he knelt. "Now I see that you'll never be able to believe in me as much as I believe in you."

Khalid shook his head violently. "You're right about most things, but you're wrong about that," he insisted. "I did trust you once, and then I stupidly let that slip away at the slightest provocation."

"Then that wasn't real trust. If you had really trusted me, why on earth would you believe I would date someone else instead of waiting for you as I'd promised? Why would you believe Amid's lies?"

Khalid frowned, and nodded his head ever so slightly at the question. "Years ago, I couldn't see why you would want to wait for me. When I found out who I really was, there was nothing in it for you. After all, I knew you weren't with me for money—and that was the only possible perk for you in this new life, in the middle of the Arabian Peninsula, a million miles away from everything you knew. I thought you'd be miserable here." Marissa started to interject, but he stopped her, raising to his full height as he did. "I know how idiotic it was to think that way now that I see you here, as much in your element as you've ever been. It's as if you were born to be a princess."

The words made her heart flutter. The thought of being Khalid's princess caused her resolve to slip. She tried to steel herself to him.

He went on. "On top of all that, I had promised to come back in four weeks. Then I let more time go by, and more. Don't you see?"

Marissa shook her head, not sure what he was saying.

"I blamed myself for what I thought was going on, all this time. And then when you told me about our baby, I blamed myself for that too."

His words cracked open the icy covering around her heart. "That makes no sense," Marissa blurted, aching for him at the thought. "Why torture yourself over something you never even knew about?"

Khalid broke eye contact and looked out into the distance before he spoke. "Because I knew, somewhere deep down, that all along I was the one forcing you away."

Marissa took in a tiny breath. What he said was true, of course, but she'd never have thought to hear him say it. She'd never even put words to it herself. He had been pushing her out of his life and then concocting all kinds of reasons to do it. All to make her fit in with everyone else in his life up to then.

"That's true," she said softly, letting her anger dissipate, feeling the love that had always been there surge again in her heart. "But," she added, as she followed her own natural conclusions to his, "that doesn't mean it was your fault that your childhood was the way it was. You didn't push your family away. That was out of your control."

Khalid brought her palm up to his lips, almost absentmindedly dropping a slow kiss on it, never taking his eyes off hers. "*Habibti*," he whispered, a glint of moisture in his dark, hooded eyes. "You've always understood me much better than I understand myself." He shook his head, swallowing hard as if trying to hold back a surge of emotion. "I know that, now. I see the difference, and I know better than to let you go, much less keep pushing you away." As if he couldn't stop himself for another second, he wrapped her up in his arms, tilted her head up to face his.

"Marissa, I don't have a ring and I don't have any right to make demands of you. So let me ask you properly, with the respect you deserve: Will you marry me? If you say yes, I promise you I will show you just how much I trust you every single day, and never let you doubt my love for you, not even for a second. Because I do love you, more than I've ever loved anyone, and I always will, no matter how you answer me right now."

Marissa's lips parted, and for a split second, even she didn't know what she was going to say. He'd reassured her, said everything she'd wanted to hear. Yet some lingering doubt remained, and as much as she wanted to, she simply couldn't chase it away. She had dreamed of this day once, even imagined it happening in an airport, just like this one. But so much had changed since then. She'd changed. Now, she needed more from Khalid than just promises.

She kept her arms wrapped around him, stayed tight in his embrace, but looked down ever so slightly. "I want to say yes," she told him, and raised her eyes back to his. "That's what's in my heart. But in my mind, I'm not sure what to do. I'm afraid, Khalid —afraid of being hurt again, after you accusing me of such outrageous things." Her voice failed her as she remembered the horrible fight that had thrown her so off-kilter.

Khalid pulled back just a fraction, nodded his head in quiet acceptance, and kissed the one tear that had somehow escaped down her cheek. "Understand this: I let myself believe all these lies because I didn't want to love you. I didn't want to do the work of loving you. I wanted our child, no doubt, I wanted you in my life. In my bed. But I never wanted to feel so raw, so vulnerable.

"I never wanted to fight the battles that come with choosing a foreign wife to bear my children, or the reality of your heart being in one country while your children were in another. I never wanted to have to face the fact that, yes, you were perfectly capable of living without me, children or not." Khalid's eyes were now glistening. "I was afraid, Marissa, of what it would mean to love you. But this month has taught me that the only fear I can't face is living without you. And let me assure you: It took me three years to get my head right the last time I distrusted you. It only took three hours this time. If I ever make the mistake again, I will give myself only three seconds of such foolishness. I give you my word."

Marissa gave up and let the tears fall.

Khalid pressed on. "Just say you'll stay a little longer. Give me a chance to prove myself to you. Because I will prove myself to you, and I will marry you, and I will make you the happiest woman in the world, if you give me a chance. I am as certain of that as I've ever been of anything in my life."

"Yes." The word hung there in the air like a tiny soap bubble, fragile and fleeting. With a silent prayer that her heart would be safe, she said it again. "Yes, I'll stay."

At that little sentence, he pulled her tightly into him and took her mouth in a kiss that made all the waiting and heartbreak and tears seem worth it. For the length of that kiss, she believed in destiny again.

But somewhere, far back in her mind, in a corner that even the touch of his lips couldn't wipe clean, a part of her was still full of fear. That part of her worried that he wouldn't ever be able to trust her in the way he would need to to make their marriage work. Part of her doubted he would always be there for her, that he would never again push her away.

And part of her knew, knew without a doubt, that time was the only way to find out.

13

That night, after they'd returned to the palace and spent a few hours just sitting on the beautiful balcony overlooking the garden, talking of anything and everything, Khalid deposited Marissa at her bedroom door with a chaste kiss and told her goodnight. At her look of surprise—and desire—he merely smiled and shook his head. "Goodnight, Marissa," he said again, with even more finality. "As much as I'd love to spend the night convincing you just how pleasurable a lifetime together could be, I know you need space to think. I've given you a lot to chew over."

Marissa pouted a moment and gave him her most come-hither look. "Are you sure?" she said in a purring voice, though she knew he was absolutely right.

"No, I am not," he said, clipped and gruff. "So you better get in there and shut the door while you still can."

She laughed and shut herself up in the bedroom, but not before collecting one more long kiss that had shivers running up and down her backbone.

The next morning, after a night of tossing and turning and

wishing she could have the comfort of Khalid's arms around her, there came a gentle knock at the balcony door.

"*Habibti*," she heard Khalid's voice whispering. "Can I come in?"

Marissa shot a look at the clock. It wasn't yet seven, and she was still in bed, incredibly drowsy from her restless night. She rolled over and propped herself up against the pillows, thinking first that she must look atrocious, and then that she didn't care—she just wanted to see Khalid. "Come in," she called, pulling herself out of bed slowly.

In a moment he was inside. "Ahh," he groaned, as he strode toward her where she was prying herself up. "You even look sexy when you're half asleep." He slipped a finger into her loose, tangled curls and ran his hands down the length of her hair. "I'm sorry to have woken you. Stay in bed. There's no need to get up, and besides, that's my favorite place for you."

His voice slipped away as he dipped in his head for a kiss that left Marissa feeling very much awake, and alive. But then he broke away. "I must leave again," he said, and the words chased all that heat out of her veins.

"What?" she said, trying to keep the panic out of her voice. "You're leaving now?" *Now, she thought, when he was supposed to be here, proving his undying love?*

He shook his head sadly. "Believe me, there's only one place I want to be right now. With you, convincing you to forgive me," he said, making her smile just a little even in the face of his bad news. "But there's a problem with the site of the new national park. We're getting word that Sheikh al Fulan is showing the area off to potential resort developers. I need to go north again and sit down with him, make sure we see eye to eye. I can't let Rifaisa lose this site. It's too precious. Too beautiful."

Marissa wrinkled her forehead, trying not to be petulant, but wanting to demand he stay. "It's just that there's so much more we should talk about, after all that's happened."

Khalid wet his lips slightly, cupped her chin in his hand. "Say the word and I'll stay. That beach is precious, but nothing is more important to me than having you by my side."

His words gave her a healthy shot of perspective. "Of course you have to go. It's your job. Your country." Marissa sighed as she reminded both him and herself that this wasn't his choice, but his duty. "It's just that—it's nothing. Never mind."

"You're scared," Khalid stated. "I've left you before and never come back."

Marissa nodded, feeling foolish but at the same time unable to deny her fears.

"I've had a wake-up call since then," he said. "And I know not to let you slip away so easily." He pressed a soft, sweet kiss to her lips to seal his words. "But the proof is in the pudding. I'll be back as soon as I can, and then you will have my full"—he pressed a kiss to the back of her neck—"complete"—another kiss dropped onto a spot just above her collarbone—"attention." And with that last word he gave her a kiss that promised a very, very attentive homecoming indeed.

But a few hours after he was gone, while the sweet sensation of his lips was still vibrating on her skin, the doubt began to creep in. She was soaking in a perfectly warm tub, the scent of roses lingering over her, when it hit her: Sheikh al Fulan. Nuriyah's father. Nuriyah might not have been the right wife for him, but she was beautiful, and she was born here. These were her people. What if Khalid saw Nuriyah and reconsidered the suitability of Marissa as a Rifaisi princess? Her stomach began to clench as her worries snowballed upon each other.

Stop it, she told herself, reminding him of everything he'd told her last night. He'd promised never to push her away again. But was that a promise he could keep? And if it wasn't, how would she know? Maybe he'd regret what he'd said the night before and decide he didn't want her for his wife.

What if he was gone for a week and came back wishing he'd

never proposed, but it was too late to undo the damage? What if he came back to her, barking about this or that person she'd spoken to on the phone or demanding to know her every move? Or worse, what if he was too proud to admit he couldn't truly trust her, and spent the rest of his life avoiding her, assuming the worst. She knew he kept another residence in Saudi Arabia for diplomatic trips, and he could live on his yacht, too. How long could he hide away this time?

Marissa shook her head fervently from side to side, sending a spray of water from her soaking hair. Even in the throes of her anxiety she could tell the difference between a reasonable concern and the spiraling doubt that came of baseless worry. But it was so hard to get a grip on her thoughts, while things seemed so uncertain and her heart was so at risk. If only they'd had more time to talk over her concerns, for her to express how scary their love felt to her.

But, she thought with a frown, even once they had some time together, would she be able to get used to all his coming and going? Did she have what it took to be the wife of a prince?

Taking a deep breath of the steamy air, she straightened her shoulders and asked herself the most important question of all: Was it worth it? Like a bell, clear and bright, the answer came to her, along with a flood of images—Khalid swimming through that bright blue-green water, the sun on his dark skin as they walked down the pristine beach, the crinkles around his eyes when he spoke of Rifaisa, or when he smiled at something she'd said. The look in his eyes when he bent his head to kiss her. Yes. Absolutely he was worth it.

And at once she understood. She had a choice: she could either believe in their love and stay here or give in to her anxiety and go. Hedging her bets, hoping to somehow protect her heart wouldn't work—love was an all-or-nothing game.

Yes, it was scary to be reminded of the way he'd left her

before, but she could handle scary. And he would come back to her. He would keep his promises.

Just like that, understanding began to resonate within her. And as if her faith had summoned him, she heard the distinctive sound of her mobile phone's text-message notification on the counter by the sink. Stepping out of the bath and toweling off, she flipped a button on the phone to see the text. It was from Khalid.

"Rest up," said the message. "You'll need your strength when I get back. And not just for ring shopping."

A shiver of happy anticipation ran over her warm, dripping body.

MARISSA WAS SWIMMING the next morning when he came back to her. Catching her breath between laps, she saw through the long glass windows a level of hustle and bustle that only could be caused by the arrival of royalty. Her heart began to pound, and she exhaled a great sigh of relief, knowing that each time he left from now on, it would get easier. He wasn't the only one who needed some practice in the trust department, she thought with a sheepish smile.

She fairly launched herself out of the pool and wrapped up in her fluffy white robe, knowing with her face red from exertion and a head full of dripping hair, she probably looked more like a melting snowman than anything else, but she didn't care. She wanted nothing more than to be wrapped up in his arms again, to feel his lips on hers, to tell him all the ideas she'd had for their wedding if he could stand to hear.

Rushing out of the glass confines of the pool room, she emerged into a long hallway and then out to the sitting area where, she thought with a shudder, she'd last lingered when Amid had urged her to depart Rifaisa forever. She wheeled around the corner and was about to plunge herself into the great room where she knew Khalid would be arriving when Jana came out of nowhere and grabbed her by the collar of her robe.

"I wouldn't go in there, if I were you," she said in a hushed voice.

"Why on earth not?" Marissa asked, thinking that Amid, the most conservative of Khalid's aides, had already seen her in a robe. What bit of protocol would she have to learn now?

Jana shook her head at Marissa, no doubt thinking she was hopeless. "Just trust me. You'll thank me later." With a nod to the great hall, Jana pulled Marissa closer to the wall where they were hidden from view. "Here, I'll show you."

As she spoke, the sound of footsteps on marble began to ring. Lots of footsteps, Marissa noticed, like a big crowd was entering.

"Who are all those people?" she asked, wondering if there was some sort of holiday or something she'd failed to research online.

"It's the royal guard," Jana whispered back, and even as she did, two men in dark suits came around the corner and gave Jana a hard look, to which she only nodded in response before they shrugged and disappeared. She tilted her head to the place where they'd been. "They're securing the area for the king."

"Abdul-Malik?" Marissa asked, incredulous. He'd been in London, she was told, for months, recovering from surgery. "He's back in Rifaisa?"

Jana nodded, her eyes looking bright with excitement. "And in very good health, I'm told."

Marissa smiled. She hadn't laid eyes on the man since that day in Las Vegas, but she remembered him being kind and empathetic. And most importantly, he was Khalid's family.

"I should go change," she exclaimed, wondering whether it would be an appropriate sign of respect to don a headscarf like she'd done on their trip to the northern beaches.

Jana read her mind. "Don't worry, I'll come up and help you figure out what to wear. If you don't mind waiting a moment? I'd love to see him."

Marissa smiled and nodded enthusiastically. "Me too," she admitted.

Just then the crowd of security personnel began to thin out and a hushed silence fell over the hall. Then came the sound of two men entering, deep in conversation. There could be no doubt in Marissa's mind whom she was listening to. Khalid's voice had an effect on her like no other.

"The bottom line," he was saying in English, "is that we will have to continue to press the issue with the old man if we want the beach to remain pristine until we are ready to announce the national park. I'll need to make a trip up there again in the next few weeks to stay on top of the situation. Politically, of course, that relationship is tenuous, so I don't think just sending a representative will do the trick."

Marissa knew he was talking about frequent trips to the house of Nuriyah's father, but she found herself less upset by that than she thought she would be. Instead she was simply happy to hear the park plans were progressing.

An older voice, clearly that of Abdul-Malik, chimed in, his voice loud and clear even around the corner where they stood. "I don't know which was the bigger mistake—forcing you to marry that woman or allowing you to annul the marriage when it didn't work." There was a hint of teasing in his voice, but still his words reminded Marissa how duty bound her future husband was, and always would be.

"Trust me, this palace is better off without her," she heard Khalid say.

"But you still need an heir."

"What I need is a wife," Khalid responded quickly. "And," he added more softly, "I have a very good candidate for that position."

"There is a woman?" Abdul-Malik asked with unmasked curiosity. Then he paused. "What is the opinion of this woman around the palace?"

"I don't intend to choose my bride by public opinion. But having said that, she is quite well liked, it seems, and no wonder. I think she will bring a great deal to our family."

At this Marissa smiled and turned to Jana, whispering, "Maybe we should give them their privacy." But before the other woman could respond, Abdul-Malik's voice cut through the silence.

"Amid, have you met this woman? What do you think of her?"

Marissa froze, and her heart, which had been beating ever faster as she heard Khalid's words, skidded to a stop. Amid was with them? She hadn't heard his voice once since they'd returned.

She knew she should leave, but she was now riveted to her spot. She leaned a little toward the great hall, to see if she could get a peek at the men, but they were still too far away.

"Your Highness, sir, I wish you would not ask that question."

Her stomach flipped over.

"Now I want to know even more, Amid. Out with it."

There was a long pause and then the unmistakable sound of Amid's low voice. "I believe she is unreliable, sir."

Stars of fury passed before Marissa's eyes. If Jana hadn't been quick enough to grab her by the shoulder and keep her in place, she would have surged right into that great hall, towel, robe and all.

Instead she was forced to stand there in silence while Amid pressed on. "She is in constant contact with an American man, and last night I heard her tell him that she was dying to return to him. It is my impression that she is using the prince, sir, and is not trustworthy."

Marissa heard his lying words and reeled at them, unable to breathe. In the hall, there was utter silence, and for a long moment her heart felt as though it was suspended in mid air, waiting for gravity to take over and smash it to pieces.

"Khalid, you must send this woman away at once." Abdul-

Malik's words brought bright hot tears to Marissa's eyes. She felt her body frozen in place, felt Jana's kind touch on her back and wondered—*does Jana trust me, at least? Or does everyone assume the worst about me? Even the man I love.*

Then Khalid did speak, and his words pulled her heart back from the precipice. "I will do no such thing. Amid, I let you stay after your last outburst because you begged me, and you were once my father's most trusted confidant. You swore you had made a mistake, and I could sympathize because I made plenty in my early years here. But now I know you are simply lying—I don't know why, and I don't care. Pack up your things and go."

Marissa's eyes popped out of her head. She had not expected that.

"*Go!*" Khalid said again, this time the word a royal decree.

There was a pregnant pause, and Marissa let herself lean forward another inch, saw Amid looking frantically between the two Abbasi men.

"You heard my grandson. You are dismissed."

"But, sir," Amid protested. "I'm only trying to protect the royal family from a deeply inappropriate arrangement. Your wife should be a Rifaisi maiden. You need someone who will secure your place here. Not an American harlot who does not know our customs."

"I strongly encourage you to watch your tongue, or you may find it incredibly difficult to find new employment in this country." Khalid's voice rumbled.

Amid responded in Arabic, his voice low and bitter enough to make Marissa glad she couldn't understand him. But she did understand the sound of his shoes stomping away, to the front door and away from her life forever. God help her, but she felt relieved.

Khalid's voice cut through her musings. "Grandfather," he began. "There will be resistance to my choice of bride, even beyond Amid's machinations. She is an American, and I know that invites speculation. There will be gossip about a trip to the States or a visit from a friend, but I've learned I can trust her with complete confidence. And I have seen in her eyes how much she will come to love our country. The ports and dunes and beaches—all have taken up residence in her heart already."

"And your heart?"

"Belongs to her. And only her," he answered, and Marissa couldn't stop the rush of tears to her eyes at those words. She had given her love to him once, and never quite gotten it back. And finally she knew it was safe in his hands.

She turned to Jana—to her friend. "Upstairs?" she whispered, knowing they had lingered long enough. A crowd of staff had gathered, from office assistants to maids, everyone straining for a look at their recovering king. But now they were looking at Marissa with admiration, and she felt every bit as desirable as Nuriyah or any other woman in the world. She grinned, and then let herself be whisked away by Jana to her bedroom, where she dressed in moments and rushed back down to greet Khalid.

When he intercepted her in the hallway that led to her bedroom, she gasped with pleasure and wrapped her arms around him, demanding a long searing kiss before either one of them said another word.

"You heard everything, I take it?" Khalid said when they finally separated. "I found quite a gathered audience in every direction when I left the great hall."

Marissa nodded. "I hope you know I didn't mean to snoop. I wanted to see you—but I wasn't dressed properly."

Khalid groaned. "I'm sorry to have missed that. You are dressed far too properly for my tastes right now."

"It's for the best," she told him, her eyes aglow with excitement. "Because I want to tell everyone in the palace what's in my heart this very instant."

He pulled back, stared deep into her eyes with undisguised joy. "So you've decided?"

Marissa laughed. "Of course! I want to marry you, Khalid. I think I always have."

He laughed too, and then pulled her to him and pressed kiss after kiss onto her forehead, her eyes, her lips, her cheeks. "Well then, come with me," he said, voice resonating with happiness. "I want my grandfather to meet my very own Rifaisi princess."

14

THE HOSPITAL WAS ABUSTLE WHEN THE HONORED GUESTS ARRIVED that evening. Marissa's mother was the first to make it in, bubbling and energetic despite the long journey from the States. Then came her cousin Natalie and brothers Knox, Carter, and Ty Madden, who had used this trip as an excuse to pursue their latest brotherly endeavor, extreme surfing, egged on by Natalie's boyfriend Charlie, a professional athlete who was afraid of nothing.

Making a more leisurely trip were Grant and Jenna and their new twins. The Blakelys had stopped overnight on each leg of the journey to make it more manageable. It was their first time in Rifaisa, though not the first time they'd seen the happy couple, since Marissa and Khalid made the trip to Las Vegas and back every time the slightest occasion warranted it.

They all made a noisy crowd, filling the halls outside Marissa's private birthing suite. Her brothers, beaming with joy, kept trying to force cigars on Khalid's hapless, nonsmoking security guards, and her mother was knitting frantically away at a beautiful blue and grey cashmere baby blanket that she'd hoped would be finished by now. After all, Marissa's labor had come a week late.

But there had just been so many other things to do besides knit—like buy everything in the baby store she could fit on a plane, and then a bit more that had to be shipped.

Now, once the nurse had given permission for visitors, it took all three of Marissa's brothers to cart in all of the beautiful flowers her family had managed to procure. And when they did, they soon found that even the Madden family couldn't compete with the royal gardener, for Khalid's gift was a towering bouquet of tea roses, in full bloom, many the size of a woman's hand. Behind all the majesty was an exhausted new mother clutching her beautiful baby boy and beaming.

"He's a stunner," said Carter as he gingerly wrapped his arms around his baby sister. For such a strong man, he was clearly terrified by the delicate little blanket full of perfection that rested in her arms. "And just on time. A few more days and we'd have missed him altogether."

Marissa laughed. "I know! I was worried that the only thing you'd see on your trip to Rifaisa is a big fat version of me. And one cool-as-a-cucumber daddy-to-be," she added, tipping her face up to smile at her amazing husband, who hadn't broken a sweat all week, despite the long delay and the bed rest she'd been through. Only she knew just how excited he was in those last few days. To everyone else he seemed the picture of a perfectly confident prince.

"I just wanted everyone healthy and happy," Khalid said. "And I have that." He leaned over at the waist and pressed a kiss on his son's forehead. "I have everything I could ever want." He moved from his new son to his wife, and whispered in her ear, "I have you, *Habibti*," and then smiled ever so slightly when he saw the shiver of pleasure flash across her face.

Suddenly there was a big ruckus at the door. "Excuse me," Marissa heard a familiar voice say in Arabic, "but I'm going in there, security sweep or not. That's my great-grandson in there!" Her face broke out in a grin. Even though her understanding wasn't one hundred percent yet, she knew enough of her new home language to know her grandfather-in-law was just as excited as everyone else to see the baby.

"Where is he?" Abdul-Malik demanded. Everyone in the room was circled around Marissa's bed as if she were the most fascinating person in the world. "Aha! There they are. The beautiful royal family," he announced in English. He made his way to the bedside, while her mother and sister fumbled with their headscarves in deference to his position. Finally he was in position to put a kiss on his grandson, and then tenderly pushed a stray hair out of Marissa's face before saying, "I'm so proud of you both."

"We are too," chimed in Marissa's mother. "You make a stunning family."

Marissa smiled, thinking that her family was indeed the most stunningly wonderful thing that had ever happened to her. And just as her husband dropped another kiss on her lips and she felt her son stir slightly in her arms, and the flashes of cameras began to fill the room as her friends and family gave in to the urge to capture the moment, she closed her eyes to take it all in.

It felt so right.

SNEAK PEEK: A TYCOON'S JEWEL

THE SIN CITY TYCOONS SERIES: BOOK 1

Can a man who came from nothing trust a woman who lost everything?

Six years ago, Jenna McCormick lost it all—her parents, her fortune, and her family's jewelry empire. After the shock wore off, Jenna realized she didn't need her fortune to be happy. Today, she has her brother's love and a small apartment. She doesn't miss the champagne lifestyle she left behind. But she can never forget the day Grant Blakely stole her family's company, placing himself at the helm. She was half in love with Grant, her father's protege, now the youngest black CEO in Las Vegas history. She never wanted to ask him for help. But now she has no choice.

When Jenna asks Grant for a job, he's certain she must be joking. Even Jenna couldn't have burned through her trust fund that fast. She's persuasive, though, and her appeal hasn't faded. Grant tests Jenna's resolve: he hires her, but as *his* assistant. She won't be able to put up with the menial tasks and hard hours of a real job. But Grant fails to predict how the sizzling attraction grows between them as he discovers she's not the playgirl she used to be.

Soon, the spark between them reignites. But can Grant trust her? And can Jenna trust the man who took everything from her?

Read on for a preview of *A Tycoon's Jewel*.

1

It took a great deal to surprise Grant Blakely. He'd seen a lot of nonsense in his position as CEO of McCormick Jewels, to say nothing of what he'd dealt with as he'd built up a real estate portfolio that covered valuable properties in Las Vegas and beyond. And then there was his father, the true master of surprise.

But walking into the waiting room outside his own office and finding the woman he'd wrestled the company away from six years ago, perched on a straight-backed chair and looking out-of-sorts—and yes, really, really good?

That was the biggest surprise he'd had in a long time.

He paused in the doorway, where he could just watch her for a moment, undetected, and leaned against the doorjamb to take in the sight. Long brown hair fell around her shoulders in pools. She drummed her fingernails on her knees and bounced her heels in and out of a pair of incredibly high-heeled, uncomfortable-looking black stilettos. She'd always been attractive, but in the last six years, she'd become an absolute knockout. She looked nervous, and seriously alluring.

Well then. Jenna McCormick, all grown up and sitting in his lobby, shaking like a doe in hunting season. Grant uncrossed his

arms, pushed himself away from the door, and cleared his throat
as he approached, enjoying the startled look on her face when she
realized he'd been watching her.

"Good morning, Ms. McCormick," he said, smooth as a cat
with a smile to match. "To what do I owe this pleasure?"

The woman—for she was certainly not the shiny-eyed party
girl she'd been the last time they'd met—jumped up out of her
chair and spun around to face him. Her large dark eyes opened
and shut tight a few times in rapid succession, as if she couldn't
believe he'd snuck up on her. When really, Grant thought, she
should have been expecting exactly that, considering their history.

He watched with some pleasure as she rearranged her
features, hiding her disarmament with a cryptic smile, as though
she'd known he was there all along. "Grant Blakely," she said,
extending a hand. "How nice to see you. It's been a long time."

Grant ignored her outstretched hand and moved past her to
the door of his office, opened it, and tried not to show his
curiosity. "Six years," he said. He moved into the office and
maneuvered around his heavy mahogany desk, knowing well
enough that she would need no invitation to follow. "Six very
prosperous years for McCormick Jewels." He dropped into his
heavy black leather chair and gestured at the trappings of the
company's newfound success.

Jenna moved to the middle of the room and took in the framed
glossy magazine covers featuring the company's most beautiful
designs and the rows of industry awards that weighed down a
glass bookshelf to his left. Her face gave away a mix of jealousy
and regret. Good. He'd brought the company a long way in the
time since she had nearly run it—and him—into the ground, and
he wasn't about to let her forget it.

"It would be hard not to notice how successful you've been,"
she said at last, though her wording made him suspect that she'd
tried. "Features in the *Times*, the *Journal*, the *Sun*. According to
Fortune you're the youngest black man to run a major corporation

in this town. And how could anyone miss the cover of *Essence's* '40 bachelors under 40' issue? I must admit, it's all very impressive. You deserve congratulations."

Grant raised an eyebrow. Though her words were polite, she seemed to be forcing them from her lips. "It sounds like you've been following my press quite closely." He leaned back in his chair and put his hands behind his head like he was sprawling on a beach chair. "I'm flattered," he said, not hiding his sarcasm, "though you're the last person I expected to deliver congratulations, considering our... history."

Jenna's expression remained controlled, but her mouth twisted just a bit at his insinuation. "If by *history* you mean the way you stole my family's company out from under me—" she began hotly, but then seemed to catch herself and started again in a much milder tone. "What I mean to say is, I do regret...that we parted on such bad terms." She turned to face him directly and gave him a polite smile. "But I'm truly glad to see the company my father worked so hard to build is doing well. He would have been very proud," she added, her smile warming just slightly.

Grant's suspicions grew. The fiery brat who'd given him such a fight the last time they'd met would never have sat across the desk from him and smiled meekly at his domination.

Unless she wanted something. "So you came in to see me today just to wish me well, then?" he asked, moving his arms to cross them in front of his chest.

Jenna faltered, just as he'd known she would. "Uh, no, not exactly."

"Oh, no? Why am I not surprised?" He leaned forward. "In that case, why don't you have a seat and enlighten me. I haven't seen or heard from you for years. What brings you to McCormick Jewels after such a prolonged absence?"

Jenna took the offered seat, a chair positioned opposite his desk, giving him a chance to fully take in the sight of her for the first time. From the moment he spotted her, it had been impossible not to notice that she'd only become more beautiful since the last time he'd seen her, her body a little less angular, her face softer and less made-up. But now he saw that there was also something different in the way she carried herself, as though she belonged here, in the corner office of a CEO. *Ridiculous,* he told himself. This was a spoiled jewelry heiress who belonged in a nightclub, not an office. It was simply her choice of wardrobe that had made him momentarily think otherwise.

She wore a smart, classically styled gray suit that was a bit conservative for a high-society bad girl, he thought, but the hem of the skirt rose just a hair over her creamy thighs, teasing him with the promise of more. He wrenched his stare away as she crossed one long curvy leg over the top of the other. *No,* Grant told himself sternly. This was not the sort of woman he could afford to indulge such thoughts about.

But she made it hard to keep up his guard. Even all those years ago, when she was refusing to step aside for the good of the company, she'd been enticing—but now, that strange pull that drew him to her was only stronger. He fought to ignore it. She was bad for business.

"I need a favor," she blurted, after a long pause. Her hands twisted in her lap with nervous energy.

Again his eyebrows shot up. "A favor? Ms. McCormick, you perplex me. When last we met, you swore you'd never speak to me again, much less ask me for a favor. Remember?" Grant let a wry smirk settle on his face. "What was it you called me again?"

At that, Jenna's lips clamped shut and her eyes shimmered. Grant couldn't miss the fire simmering beneath her forced composure. He had to admit, he was enjoying watching her squirm. Perhaps more than he should.

"I really couldn't recall," she said, clearly trying to tamp down her temper and play nice. "But I'm sure I said it in the heat of the moment. My parents had just died, if you'll remember, and I was in shock—"

"Let's see…" Grant interrupted, drumming his fingers on the desk. "I believe you called me a morally corrupt, scheming cheat who'd drive this business into the ground." Now his smile grew larger. "That's right. A morally corrupt, scheming cheat. Now why would you ask a favor from such a person?"

Jenna took a deep breath and shook her head, as though regrouping her resolve. Against his better judgment, Grant found himself intrigued by her unwillingness to give in to her emotions. Such a change from the last time he'd seen her. "Please understand, when I said that, I was under a lot of strain. My parents had just died. And I—" she looked upwards for a moment, as if searching for the right words, "I had just lost the thing that mattered most in the world to them. There's no way you could have known this at the time, but I had promised my father I would always keep a hand in this company, no matter what." Her eyes drifted downward. "That day was when I realized I would have to break that promise."

Grant shook his head, unwilling to give her even the tiniest bit of sympathy. "The way I remember it, you had some choice in the matter. In fact, if memory serves, as soon as you stopped your little tirade that day, I offered you a chance to stay. An entry level job, so you could learn the business the right way. You threw it back in my face so fast I didn't even get to finish my sentence."

He remembered that day perfectly. She'd just found out about the board's decision to choose him over her as the new CEO, and she'd barged into his office, mad as a wet hen, and read him the riot act. Despite his annoyance, he'd felt duty-bound to promise her a job at the company—starting at the bottom, of course—if she ever saw fit to join the rest of the working world. Which, he felt quite sure, she never would.

She'd merely laughed at his offer and told him exactly where he could stick it as she stormed out.

Jenna cleared her throat. "I was too hasty then," she said, as if such an understatement could describe her childish behavior.

"But I had hoped, after all this time, that we might put the past behind us," she said in a cool, almost detached voice. "And that you might help me out of respect for my father. I'm sorry if I've made a mistake."

Grant snorted. "If our situations were reversed, if you were in my shoes, would you have time for a favor for me?"

Her eyes lost focus for a moment at that, as though she were imagining herself sitting at his desk, heading up the company she'd wanted so badly to lead six years ago. So badly she'd nearly ruined his career, and the company's reputation with it. He watched her carefully, wondering how she could possibly respond.

When she did speak, her voice sounded resigned, almost sad. "I can't imagine you ever needing a favor from me," she said softly.

The words found their target, and Grant felt that twinge of guilt. It was true, he was a self-made businessman and his success was all his own. And she—she was a former heiress with nothing but her social connections to fall back on. She probably needed all the help she could get.

He sighed, rubbing a hand through his black hair. "Look, you're right about one thing. Your father was a good mentor to me. If I can help you, I will, even though you surely don't deserve it. But you'll have to get on with it. I'm a very busy man, and I have no interest in sitting around rehashing old times. At least, not with you."

JENNA'S HEART WAS POUNDING. Though she'd thought through her dilemma every which way and sideways, she hadn't been able to think of a better solution than the one she was about to suggest. This solution wouldn't exactly keep her promise to her father, of course, but it would be something, something that she knew he would be proud of if he were still alive. It would serve as the proof that she would never again let go of the family business, even if she was only holding on by the thinnest of threads. Proof that she wouldn't abandon what the McCormicks had worked so hard to create.

But as badly as she wanted to do right by her family, the moment she'd laid eyes on Grant Blakely again, her fortitude had left her, and she'd wished desperately to be anywhere but there. She'd known going in that it would be hard seeing *him* again. He was the man who had shattered her fantasies about life. He'd stolen her family's business only a few weeks after she'd become, well, an orphan. He'd heartlessly let her twist in the wind. And he still believed she'd deserved it.

She'd prepared herself to be reminded of what had happened the last time she was in his office, the pain of that day and everything that led to it. But she hadn't been prepared for one added wrinkle.

The man who had been her adversary back then had only become more attractive with time, looking every bit the wildly successful power broker he'd become. She could see now why his name showed up so often in the tabloids, attached to this or that model, spotted in some glitzy casino with high rollers. In his impeccably tailored suit, he towered over her, every inch of him solid and immovable, from his dark sculpted jaw to the broad expanse of his shoulders. He'd been formidable enough the last time she'd seen him, but now? She was way out of her depth, and she knew it. Her body trembled with awareness as she took him in. And the way he was looking at her—his piercing brown eyes raking over her like he wanted to eat her alive—didn't make pleading her case any easier.

She could apologize to him for wasting his time and bolt, she thought. She could race out the door and never set foot in this building again, forget the business her father and mother had built together, as a team, the business they would have entrusted to her if they'd had the chance.

But she couldn't forget her brother. She closed her eyes and thought of him, and it kept her seated in that office, kept her face neutral, kept her from showing all the trepidation she felt sitting this close to Mr. Grant Blakely, CEO of her father's company. A man who was, for the second time in her life, in control of her destiny.

She swallowed hard. "Grant, I know we've had our differences in the past," she said, biting her tongue on all the things she truly wanted to say about how he'd treated her the last time they'd met. "And it's not easy for me to ask for it, so you must know how badly I need your help. You see, I'm…I'm in a tight spot. Financially. And I miss this company—"

"I'll bet you do. It must have been quite a nice source of cash when your father was in charge."

Ignore him and stick to the speech, Jenna reminded herself, though inwardly she seethed at his accusation. Ignoring someone whose presence dominated the room the way Grant's did wasn't easy. "Six years ago you offered me a chance to work here. Promised me a job if I wanted it. I am wondering if you'd still be willing to hire me after all this time. Please. I need a job—any job —as soon as possible."

There. It was out of her mouth. Had she begged? She'd tried so hard to keep the desperation out of her voice. Dignity was all she had right now.

But Grant merely laughed. "Now you want a job? You? Jenna McCormick? Please tell me this is some sort of joke." He laid his arms flat on his desk like a sphinx, leaning in as though he couldn't believe this was happening. Almost like he was angry. *Offended,* even. A shiver ran up her spine.

"I'm quite serious." She leaned right back into the desk, suppressing her anger but not letting herself back down. "I want to come back here and work. For you."

Grant shook his head, but didn't lean back. "Ask for anything else. Ask for money—I can write you a check. Ask for an apartment—one of my holdings can surely hold the likes of you. Hell, ask for a setup with one of my rich older friends. I'll find you a sucker *and* lend you the jewelry for your first date."

"A date?" Jenna recoiled, stung. "A *date*?" Now he had pushed her too far. "You think a date with a wealthy man is the same as a job?" She stopped herself before she completely lost her temper and risked forfeiting her only chance at getting back on her feet, but her pride burned. Did he think she was for sale?

Grant only raised his eyebrows, didn't back down an inch—in that regard, he hadn't changed at all. "Maybe I'm wrong, Ms. McCormick. Maybe you're too proud to be a gold digger. But let me ask you this: How old are you?"

You know exactly how old I am, she thought. She'd been twenty-one when her parents passed away. Just old enough to legally take control of the company, though in her heart, she knew she'd been far too young for the responsibility. "I'm twenty-seven."

He shook his head. "Twenty-seven years old now. And you've been doing exactly what since we last met? Working your way up from the mailroom at a Fortune 500 company, learning the ropes and putting in your dues? Or maybe getting a college degree and applying for your MBA?"

"Not exactly," said Jenna, hating the direction this was going. "I've had commitments."

"Right. I can guess what's been occupying your time, and I know it's not business school. If you're coming to me looking for a job, that must mean you've blown through your trust fund and are looking for a meal ticket. But you don't want to go work just anywhere, do you?" Grant shook his head with something that looked like disgust. "You want to work at Daddy's company so you can coast during the day and you won't risk missing out on your valuable pedicure time. Isn't that right, Jenna?" He said her name like it was a foul taste in his mouth, and she was reminded of just how cruelly he'd laughed at her the last time she'd been in his office. How devastated she'd been that day.

"With all due respect, this has nothing to do with pedicures," Jenna said, unable to remember the last time she'd seen the inside of a spa. "I can work hard, and I will—because I have responsibilities." Responsibilities that were none of Grant Blakely's business.

"I can only imagine. A responsibility to our community's retail outlets. You probably single-handedly propped up the Las Vegas economy with the purchase of that outfit and the diamond watch you're wearing."

At the mention of her mother's watch, Jenna's anger simmered over. Who was this man to think he knew who she was, to accuse her of being a dumb, spoiled brat, when he knew nothing about her life? He didn't have the first idea what it was like to lose everything she'd held dear when she was barely old enough to know her own mind. He didn't know how hard it had been to see her brother on the edge, day in and day out, always on the brink of disaster—and then, that horrible day, over the brink.

Grant Blakely didn't need—didn't deserve—to know anything about her.

Could she put up with this imperious man for her family? Once more she pressed her eyes closed, tried to summon up thoughts of her father, her mother, and her brother's smiling face.

It worked. Her family always gave her power. She summoned her strength and rose to her feet, advanced around the mahogany desk that probably cost more than a year's rent in her run-down apartment, and positioned herself right in front of Blakely—just exactly as he'd done to her six years ago. "I know what you think about me—what you've always thought of me," she said, trying to keep her voice from shaking. "But please understand, I am not some trust-fund brat—or I'm not anymore. I can work, I can start from the bottom, I can make coffee and book calendars and take phone messages. I am very capable of working in an office, and doing it well. I just need someone—I need *you*—to give me a chance."

Her voice softened, and she looked him right in the eye so he would see how much she meant the words she said. "If you do, I promise you will not regret it."

For just a moment, the smirk on Grant's handsome face was replaced by contemplation. And then, slowly, his mouth bent into a wide, wicked grin, a grin that sent tremors of fear up and down Jenna's spine. He leaned back in his chair to angle his face upward toward her. "You want a job that badly? You think you can do the work? Fine. I promised you a job, and you will have one—for three months. After that I will evaluate you, see if your performance is up to par. There are no free rides at McCormick Jewels—or at least there haven't been in six years."

Jenna was so relieved that he was hiring her that she ignored his dig and took a deep breath instead. "Thank you, Grant. Thank you so much." She fought the urge to reach across the desk and touch his arm, reminding herself to be a professional. This was her big chance. Her only chance.

"Don't thank me just yet," said Grant. As he rose, he reached out and touched—practically caressed—her chin, and tilted her face to look right into those dangerous blue eyes. "I didn't tell you what your job would be. I need a new personal assistant—I've been using temps for months—and you're it. From now on, you work directly under me."

2

"UNDER YOU?" FOR A LONG MOMENT, JENNA WAS UNABLE TO DO
more than repeat the words. There, standing so close to this
powerful man, she felt a charge between them she'd never felt in
her life. Her mind went blank, then flashed to an image of herself
literally *under* his body that was so torrid she had to shake her
head to get back to reality. Where had *that* come from? "I don't
want to sound ungrateful, but that makes no sense."

"Oh, no?" Grant asked, his voice low, intense. His eyes were
fixed on her. Could he be feeling the strange electricity, too?

"None whatsoever." She had to talk him out of this. Working
in such close proximity with this man was beyond contemplation.
"You just said yourself that I'm inexperienced, a novice, have no
idea what it means to work hard. Why would you want to have to
personally deal with that every single day?"

Grant broke his gaze at last, and glanced toward the door, as if
assessing their level of privacy. "Because, Ms. McCormick, I want
you where I can see you. What you say is true: I don't think you're
capable of hard work. So why would I want to impose you on any
of my prized employees? You'll find that incompetence"—on that
word, his gaze swung right at her, ran up and down her form like

he was shopping for a new suit, or a fast car—"incompetence is not welcome here, and I refuse to subject my colleagues to anything of the sort. You'll work under me."

Oh, that phrase again, and the imagery that came with it. "At least until your evaluation," he finished. "At which point I suspect this matter will be brought to a close."

At that, Jenna's earlier terror morphed into irritation. *The arrogant bastard.* He thought she was such a brainless twit that no one but him would be able to put up with her? How little he knew! She couldn't wait to set him straight, to show him just how capable she could be.

But wait. Since when did she care what Grant Blakely thought of her? She'd wanted this job so that she could afford to take care of her brother, and to keep one foot in the McCormick family business, such as it was. She wasn't doing this to impress the very man who'd stolen the company from her. She'd sworn never to speak to him again, much less to stand so close to him…to feel such an intensity oozing from his body…to have the urge to touch every inch of him with her burning fingertips…

"I have to go," she blurted. She had to get away from him before her mind raced off somewhere her body couldn't follow. All the fight was out of her, replaced by an unstoppable urge to flee. "I have, um, I have someplace to be. Thank you so much for the job. I won't let you down."

Grant pulled back from his close stance, turned away from her, and she felt instantly dismissed. It stung. "Just as I suspected," he said. "Wouldn't want to keep the pedicurist waiting. But starting tomorrow, you're mine from nine in the morning until I say so in the evening, and you should know how late this business can require you to work. So many working dinners and client receptions…" Again he looked her up and down, and her blood sizzled. "Though perhaps you'll shine in that arena. Clear your schedule. This time tomorrow, you belong to me."

THE MOMENT JENNA MCCORMICK left his office—well, *fled* was probably a more apt word—Grant sat down and ran his fingers aggressively over his close-cropped dark hair, as if he was trying to force something from his brain.

Who was that woman? She was not the 21-year-old debutante he'd once known, not by a long shot. That girl had been demanding and pouty, the product of a mother who couldn't say no to anything and a father who offered her the world. When her parents had died, she'd seemed put out to return to Vegas from her ski trip in Tahoe, as though there was still fun to be had whether her mother and father were above ground or below it.

Grant frowned at the memory of that dark day. She'd marched into this office, skis in hand, as though she expected to find her father still there. He would never forget the fit she'd thrown when she'd found him sitting in the CEO's office instead, organizing the files he'd brought from the smaller VP's office to this one. It was one of the worst days in his life. He'd been lost in grief for his mentor, and daunted by his sudden responsibility to the company. Which, he supposed, had included her.

And yet still, even back then, there'd been no denying a flicker of attraction between them. She was absolutely wrong for him in a million ways, but it was no use telling that to his body. He'd fought tooth and nail to keep himself focused on business. And it was a good thing, too. If he hadn't, perhaps she'd have succeeded at taking over the company. And bankrupting them all.

He remembered her frantic attempts to turn the board of directors against him six years ago, and disdain surged through him. He'd tried to make it easier on her back then. Though technically she'd been old enough to take control of her father's share of the business, she was nowhere near mature enough to handle the responsibilities of running a Fortune 500 company in the nation's most power-hungry city. Her own father had known that. And right away Grant had offered her a way out—one that involved a family partnership on the board, but no active control in the company. But that hadn't suited her whims. She had fancied herself a CEO at twenty-one, and, egged on by a vast team of lawyers, she'd been willing to risk ruining the company's stock value to make it so.

Grant shook his head at her foolishness. Her impulsive move could have rendered all his work and his hard-won reputation in business completely worthless. She had broken a cardinal rule of corporate power: Never risk something you're unwilling to lose. She'd given up her controlling shares in McCormick in an attempt to win favor with the board, and the risk hadn't paid off. Liquidating shares so soon after the tragedy had brought down prices and lost them all money, and the company had been barely afloat as it was. The very next day, she was fired by the board, pure and simple, and without the controlling stock holdings, there was nothing left to tie a single McCormick to the company the family had built from the ground up.

It must have been a rough day for Jenna McCormick. That was the day she'd stormed into the big office and declared him a "morally corrupt, scheming cheat who would drive the company into the ground." And the day he'd made a offhand promise to hire her if she was ever willing to work.

A promise that now, after all this time, was coming back to bite him.

Grant sighed, thinking of everything that had happened since he'd made that offer. As CEO, he had helped the company turn a vast profit by the second year. His resulting bonuses had been the beginning of an empire. He pivoted in his chair and looked out the huge windows of his office onto the flashing lights of the Vegas strip. A bit of it even belonged to him. He was welcome at every VIP room in every casino in town. He never had to wait for a table at Bouchon. Thanks to his work ethic and good fortune, having a woman show up at his door looking for a handout was nothing new. But today, Jenna hadn't wanted a handout.

Had she changed? Growing up into that tempting body of hers, with her long, curvaceous legs and lips like invitations, had she grown up emotionally, too?

Nonsense. Grant forced himself to ignore the tightening sensation at the thought of her body and concentrate instead on what might have happened had Jenna taken control of the company successfully. She'd have ruined his reputation and that of McCormick Jewels as well. The last he'd heard of her had been a year after the takeover, and she'd been smoothing her ruffled feathers at the best suite in the Venetian, interviewing doctors in top-secret private meetings. Which possibly explained where those incredible breasts had come from…

Stop thinking about her breasts, he scolded himself. *Remember the real reason she's here.*

For Grant knew that Jenna McCormick hadn't shown up in his office begging for a job just because she needed money. He'd offered her a position so unappealing she'd have been crazy to take it over any number of overpaid, underworked ladies-who-lunch gigs she could have gotten from her parents' connections. And besides, her parents had left her with enough money that she should have gotten away with her life of leisure for many more years. So why here? Why now?

The penny dropped.

She was husband hunting. He didn't want it to be true, but he'd known plenty of heiresses and gold-diggers in this strange gilded city. They shopped for pro athletes and CEOs the way some people shopped for shoes. Why would Jenna be any different?

He thought back to the moment he'd described the position to her. "You will work directly under me," he'd said. Under him. Her reaction hadn't been the disgust he'd expected. Actually, her whole body had seemed to sizzle at the words. Was it sexual attraction, pure and simple, or something more calculating?

Of course. What better way for her to keep that promise she'd made to her father to keep a hand in the company. She'd weasel her way into his life, and never have to work a day again, but still enjoy all the spoils of McCormick Jewels' success. The thought went against everything Grant believed in.

He thought again of her pleading eyes. Her nervous demeanor. He wanted more than anything to be wrong about her. But he was so seldom wrong about anyone. He'd learned long ago that trusting his gut without doing all of his research was dangerous. It was not a mistake he ever intended to repeat. He had to be sure.

He buzzed his assistant. "Anna?" he said to the latest in a string of temps manning his front desk. "Get me James Houghton, please."

"Frames who now?" came a distracted voice.

Grant sighed. "James Houghton. As in Houghton Investigatory Services. I've got some digging to do."

"Hello? Who is this?"

Grant could tell by the drowsy way Jenna answered the phone that he had woken her. Good. After all, thoughts of her had kept him up half the night, and he was happy to return the favor. "Good morning, Jenna."

"Grant? I mean, Mr. Blakely? Why are you calling me at 6:15 in the morning?"

"It's not too early, is it?" he asked in mock innocence. "I hope you're up and moving, because I need you here soon. I've arranged a 7:30 meeting today, and I'd like you to be around to greet the attendees."

There was a short silence on the line, and then she spoke. "Seven-thirty in the morning?"

"Absolutely. The best work gets done while everyone is still fresh, wouldn't you agree?" Grant grinned as he spoke. Considering he was in his pajamas, sipping from an oversize mug of French roast as he looked through his picture windows at the waking city below, this was as fresh as it got.

"I've never thought anything but bagels should be fresh at 7:30 in the morning," she quipped. But she added in a much more professional voice, "Sorry. I'll be there by 7:30 on the dot. I'd appreciate it if you could try to give me a little more warning in the future, though, if you don't mind. I need forty-five minutes to make the commute."

"Oh, you're that close to the office, then?" Grant shot back. "In that case, why don't you come in a little earlier, so you have time to brew a big pot of coffee for the meeting? I take mine black. No sugar." He heard a muffled squawk on the other line, like someone had just dropped an anvil on her toe, and for a brief moment he pitied her. A lifetime without lifting a finger. Working for a taskmaster would be a terrible shock, he knew.

But the moment passed. If she wanted to play at being an employee, he could show her just how demanding some bosses could be. Never mind that he'd worked with his last permanent assistant, a college grad named Nate, for five years without a single complaint. Never mind that Nate had accused him of being a softie when it came to days off and family issues. Jenna would get to know the more intense side of life as a personal assistant. After all, she was the one who wanted to get *really* personal.

ON THE OTHER end of the line, Jenna squeezed her eyes shut, then open, then shut again. One more time and maybe she'd be transported back to her bed, sleeping dreamlessly, instead of standing here seething at her new boss. *Tyrant* was more apt a title for the man. Of course he took his coffee dark and bitter—just like his personality. How could she have ever felt attracted to him? Now that he was almost an hour away, it was much easier for her to remember her previous resentment for the hard-hearted man.

A quick shower was all she had time for. Then she slid into the same dark gray suit she'd worn to meet him yesterday, with a different silk top—she'd never had much need for business attire in her old life, and would have to get by on two suits mixed and matched—and went looking for a hairbrush to try to force her long, brown, stick-straight hair into a respectable shape of some sort. She found it lying in front of a framed photo of her whole family, taken in easier times.

Good. She slid the photograph into her tote bound for the office. It was the perfect reminder of why she was doing this today. She'd go in there with her head held high and her arms full of coffee mugs, ready to dazzle the tyrant's fine Italian trousers right off. Wait—scratch that. She didn't want to think about his trousers off for even a second. But it was too late. The image of a long muscular pair of legs squeezed its way into her head before she could stop it. And then a picture of those legs twisted with hers in the sheets…

No, Jenna Lynn McCormick! Absolutely not, she scolded herself, shaking her shoulders to set her head right. *Do not think about your new boss that way. Brush hair, put on lipstick, get in car, drive to new job.* She barked out instructions to herself as she got to each step, as if to speed herself along. Or force herself forward.

Within fifteen minutes she was in the car, pulling out of the driveway of the little concrete apartment block that she'd come to think of as her "little Bellagio." It wasn't anywhere near as grand as the real thing, where she'd crashed regularly before her parents died, but she liked it whole heck of a lot better. Oh, she hadn't at first—she'd acted like a brat, like a poor little rich girl, and stormed about expecting the world to hand her back her old life.

But now she enjoyed the simplicity and privacy of her cozy home. And the security it provided.

As she sped toward the twinkling lights and commanding buildings of the Strip, she thought again of how she'd gotten to this place—how her routine had gone from ski trips and spa days to a quiet existence in North Vegas, taking care of herself and her little brother, trying not to think too much about what came next. It wasn't bad at all—in fact she rather loved her peaceful, humdrum life. Truly, everything would have been perfect if she hadn't had so many expenses. But the money worries had just gotten to be too much, and every day that her wallet got lighter, her heart got heavier. She hated waking up in the morning and wondering how she'd pay for a tank of gas that day—or, more importantly, how she'd make sure her brother continued to get the inpatient care he needed.

When her parents had died, she'd known absolutely nothing about managing money. Now she knew all too well the ins and outs of preserving each nickel as long as she could. But it was too little, too late. The expense of her brother's illness had quickly drained the bulk of the trust funds left by her parents, and soon they were living on the capital. When that was gone, they'd sold the house and all its contents at auction. Thanks to her father's shrewd real estate sense and her mother's taste for rare collectible art, that was enough to keep Justin in good care for however long he might need it, as long as Jenna never touched a penny of the money. And to ensure that she wouldn't, she'd faced her fears and returned to the company that had burned her so badly six years ago.

From behind a line of standstill road congestion, the Wynn hotel at the top of the Strip slowly came into view, and with a wry smile, Jenna remembered how lucky she'd been—how good she'd had it, though she hadn't realized at the time. A suite at the Bellagio, endless vacations, every pair of shoes Barney's had ever carried. It was enough to make her shake her head and laugh at herself. What kind of dope would take all the riches of the world for granted, spend her days sleeping and nights dancing, instead of going to the best schools and learning the business that had given her such a good life? Ah, but she'd beaten herself up about that long enough. Time to face life as it was. Time to move on from the regret and sorrow and get to the business of making things better.

Traffic was miserable, and by the time she reached the office, it was already 7:15. She ran from the underground parking garage beneath the building to the elevator and then shot up seventeen agonizing floors almost without taking a breath. She bolted to the empty reception desk just outside of Grant's office—she guessed it had to be her post—and before she'd even thrown down her jacket and purse, she saw the message light on the phone blinking back at her.

At first she tried to ignore it, to rush through to the next task. She still had time to find the coffee maker and get at least one pot going before the meeting started. But what if it was Grant, adding to his orders? Jenna sneered. What could he possibly want? Handmade scones to go with the coffee?

She lifted the receiver, already regretting the precious moments she was losing, and pressed the play button. The unmistakable voice of Grant Blakely came on the line: "Looks like you have time for a pedicure after all." His voice was booming, triumphant. "That is, if you can find a salon that's open at 7:30 in the morning. I pushed back the meeting. Your reluctant tone made me realize that the hour was far too early to get any real work done. We'll reconvene at nine a.m. Keep the coffee warm, please." The tell-tale click sounded, letting her know no further instructions would be forthcoming.

Jenna wanted to scream—but what came out when she opened her mouth was a mangled, anguished gurgle. That unbelievable *jerk*. There'd never been a 7:30 meeting. He was toying with her on her first day, trying to drive her so crazy she'd have to quit before she even started. Rousing her hours too early and making her race into the office without so much as breakfast? Scaring her half to death that her job was on the line? How could he be so smug? Again, she scolded herself for letting the man's obvious attractiveness distract her for even a moment from his true nature.

At that moment, she wanted nothing more than to grab her purse, march right back to her car, and go home to hide from the world—and especially from Grant Blakely. But instead, Jenna rolled her shoulders back in her characteristic way, took one of her deep breaths, and reminded herself what she was doing this for.

Clearly, this arrogant man thought she'd give up after a few little frustrations and then he could be rid of her. Well, he didn't know her well enough. He didn't know how her father had made her promise to always keep a hand in the jewelry company, no matter what happened, even when she was just a little girl and had no idea what the words had meant. He didn't know her brother needed special care and was counting on her to keep it coming.

If Grant Blakely wanted to break her, he was welcome to keep trying. What he didn't know was that she'd sooner break than give up on her family.

3

Jenna's first meeting went off without a hitch. At nine a.m. sharp, the conference room filled with men and women in fine suits, holding yellow notepads and looking Jenna up and down with undisguised curiosity. She stood at the door and introduced herself to each newcomer, trying to make the best possible impression on each of Blakely's prized employees in the hope of earning their respect. Most attendees were friendly and welcoming, and some knew her from her father's tenure. But more than a few asked after her last name, wondering aloud at the relationship between the company and herself. When they did, she just smiled warmly and explained as best she could that yes, she was in the McCormick family, but was just starting out and wanted to learn about the business from the ground up, paying her dues like everyone else.

That explanation earned her more than a few approving nods, but a couple of the staff members merely turned away from her, as though they didn't believe what she'd said. Probably, like Grant, they thought she was a freeloader, here in search of a cushy job with time for long lunches. Jenna tried to let it roll off her back. They'd see soon enough that wasn't the case.

Grant arrived last, surprising her by appearing from behind the door of his office, which had been closed all morning. She greeted him professionally, hoping that strange pull she felt each time she laid eyes on him wasn't as obvious to him as it was to her.

Had he actually arrived at the office even earlier than she? Yes, Jenna realized, he'd been back there all this time, just a few feet away, while she had struggled to learn the phone system, tried to find her way around the building, and readied the conference room for the meeting. Could he have been *less* helpful?

Or perhaps more busy, she corrected herself. She remembered how hard her father had worked as CEO, especially at this time of year, before the International Jewelers Organization conference that descended on Las Vegas each June and turned the business upside down. Watching Grant in his smart, handmade suit as he crossed to the head of the conference table, she thought of the late nights and early mornings he probably spent hunched over stacks of diamond orders and new designs, pondering the best marketing for a tennis bracelet or a pendant necklace like the one she wore now, a single luminescent solitaire that had been her 21st birthday present from her father.

It was a big job, and without wanting to, Jenna had to give Grant credit for the success he'd found in it. She watched and took minutes from a chair off to the side as he guided the staff through the meeting, easily managing different personalities and handling issues large and small. As hard as she tried not to, she found the balance of warmth and efficiency he used in handling his staff most impressive.

If only he could have been so fair and kind six years ago, when he'd handled her.

When the meeting was over, Jenna hustled back to her desk, hoping to at least be able to get comfortable on the phones and set up her email account before Grant assigned her another task. But she'd only managed to turn the computer on and create a login before he strode into the room, a bold smile on his face and a thick pile of sketches in one hand. On his arm, he'd draped his suit coat, and in just his tailored white shirt and tie, the defined muscles of his arms and chest were all too apparent. Jenna tried, unsuccessfully, not to notice. If there was a single man in the world she shouldn't be attracted to, it was Grant Blakely.

"From the design team," he said, moving assuredly toward his office and waving the stack of papers in the air. "I need you in my office to take notes while I brief before the meeting at one. I haven't had a chance to become familiar with the Series 5 and 6 rings, and the designers will know the moment I walk in if I'm unprepared. I've got to cram, or I'm in serious danger of wasting other people's time."

Jenna was surprised to hear him confess his unreadiness to her. The admission almost made him seem human. Was that what made him so successful in business, this disarming openness that won you over at the word go? It certainly did make her want to work harder, to try to make him happy.

Jenna shook her head to clear it of such a romantic notion. Everything Grant Blakely did was manipulation, pure and simple. She remembered how he had behaved six years before, when she'd been at her lowest. First he'd seemed like a friend she could trust—and then he'd pounced. He'd never been willing to admit any wrongdoing then, and now he was just using this nice-guy demeanor to get what he wanted.

She couldn't let down her guard, no matter how approachable —make that irresistible—he might seem.

"I'm sure I can help," she said, squelching the bubbles of emotion that ran through her as best she could. She followed him into his office, sat on the couch off to the side of his desk with her notepad balanced on her knees, and looked up at her new boss. "I'm ready when you are."

But he wasn't ready. He was standing beside his desk chair, frozen, staring down at her hotly—almost as if he was angry. Or was she mistaking intensity for anger? Jenna stared back, trying to return the look he was giving her. It was almost as if he could stare into her head and see her thoughts. What did he imagine they were? And what was he thinking in return?

She hoped his thoughts weren't as licentious as hers were quickly becoming. Under his searing gaze, with his brown eyes and heavy lashes fixed on her, her whole body seemed to loosen and turn into liquid. She blinked hard, trying to break the connection between them.

But it was useless. He didn't avert his stare, only squared his shoulders to face her, as though he might reach out one hand to pull her in, to press his body against hers. That simple action was too much for Jenna's vivid imagination. She felt her defenses go slack, and her shoulders dropped as if her spine was molten. With all her might, she willed him to look away—even as her body sent images to her mind of him crossing the room, pushing her down on the couch, opening her suit jacket and sliding his hand across the planes of her bare chest. How warm his hand would feel, how it would burn her skin as it moved under the strap of her camisole, pushing it down, moving his head lower for a kiss.

Just like that, his eyes released their lock on hers and dropped to the papers on his desk. It was as if a spell had been broken. How long had that moment lasted? A second? A minute? An hour? Had she imagined it altogether?

"Jenna? Are you with me?"

Jenna flushed. She hadn't imagined it. Or rather, she had imagined all too much, and left herself staring at her new boss like a starstruck fan. Had her mouth been open? She shuddered at the thought. *Be a professional,* she reminded herself.

"I apologize, Grant." She poised her pen over the notepad and crossed her legs. She caught him watching one leg slide over the other and felt a frisson of awareness. "You need to review the new designs?"

"Right. Lets start with the newest rings. Take notes, please—I prefer to think aloud." He picked up a manila folder full of sketches. "I asked the designers for a look that was more art deco than what we've done in the past for engagement rings. We need to take back lost business from online estate dealers. Come over here and take a look."

Jenna blanched, then forced herself to cross to the desk, lean over the opposite side. "No, come over *here*." He waved an arm toward himself. "Many of these rings have a right side and a wrong side. You can't look at them from upside down and get a real impression."

Obediently, she rounded the desk, wedged herself behind it, standing just inches from where he leaned forward in his executive chair, close enough that she could feel the heat from his body. She leaned over the plans and tried to think businesslike thoughts. "Look at 6B," Grant instructed. "What's the problem there?"

Jenna stared at the ring, tried to clear her mind. But only one answer would pop into her head, so she blurted it out. "It's unattractive?"

She was afraid her comment might offend him, but instead Grant laughed, a warm, lit-up sound Jenna found a little surprising and incredibly disarming. "Well. I suppose it might be. But that's not the biggest issue. Here." He reached out his right hand towards hers, and for a bated moment she thought he was about to take her hand. Instead, he slipped the pen she'd been holding out of her fingers to circle a portion of the design in ink. Jenna felt the heat of his glancing touch echo on her skin even after it was gone. "See these diamonds?" He ran the pen over the side diamonds that flanked the center stone—first the left, then the right. "Look how big they are in comparison to the center stone."

"Very big. And therefore expensive," Jenna said, nodding as she caught on. "The customer—presumably a man getting ready to propose—will want to spend his money on the biggest center stone he can afford, and save on the rest of the setting."

"That's exactly right." There was energy in his voice. No matter what his pretense, she couldn't doubt he loved this business. "According to our market research, male jewelry shoppers are often looking for bragging rights. Total carat weight tends to make their eyes glaze over. They're looking for one big impact—the thing that will make her say yes."

Jenna heard the words, let them echo in her head, stopped herself before her mouth formed the word "yes" back at him. She cleared her throat. "Did you say this ring was 6B?"

"Yes." Grant looked back to his paperwork, as though he too were remembering himself. "Now, the other rings in the 6 series," he droned, while she scribbled notes along. "I like them. I need more originality on A, C , and D, but E is a selling ring." He paused while Jenna took his thoughts down, then shuffled to a new set of pages. "The 5 series I've seen a few times now, and I think it's getting to where it needs to be. This is the look for women interested in colored diamonds."

"Fancies." Jenna murmured the industry lingo without thinking. "Yellow, champagne, blue, pink."

"Yes, although champagne is a saturated market at the moment. The trick is, the fancy diamonds are so expensive in the popular colors that the rings need to be designed to accommodate smaller solitaires. Or settings with fewer side stones to keep them affordable."

Jenna nodded, understanding almost by instinct the challenge that presented. "But they still need to look dazzling and unique," she said. "Look at this one, 5C. Does it ring any bells for you?"

Grant looked up at her curiously, wondering what she might have to say. "Only because I've reviewed this design several times. I liked this one from the word go."

"It looks very familiar." She spoke without thinking. "I think it's quite similar to a new Tiffany design."

Grant's brow furrowed, surprised at her observation, and in response, Jenna's confidence soared. Maybe she wouldn't always be tipped off balance when they were together. At the moment it almost felt as though they were relating to each other as equals.

"Yes. I'm quite sure of it," she went on. "It's almost identical." Though she hadn't spent a dime on jewelry since her brother's diagnosis, she had let herself linger at the windows of her second favorite designer now and then.

Grant took in what she was saying and then uttered a cold, sharp laugh. "I'm not surprised that you're familiar with the competition's inventory," he retorted quickly. The words held a sting, and they found their target. He pushed himself back from the desk, rose to standing—tall, commanding, ready again to pounce. Jenna felt herself deflate in his shadow.

"Pull up the matching ring on the Tiffany website," he said, after a moment's consideration. "I don't doubt your claim for a second, but I need to be prepared when I discuss this with my designers." He rubbed his angled jawline and frowned. "It's a serious issue, you know. Of course legal would have caught it, but by then we might have wasted a portion of the Series 5 budget on development and research. Besides, cutting corners like this is not what McCormick Jewels is known for." Grant looked right at Jenna with this last bit and scowled. "At least, not anymore."

Her blood boiled. For a fleeting second she'd felt so proud of herself—she'd noticed something important that others had missed, saved the company money, done good work for the first time in her life, and on her very first day! But with just a sentence, Grant Blakely had changed that pride to bitter scorn. Her eyes narrowed, but she held tight to her dignity. She turned away from him, injured, but unwilling to let it show.

"I'll see to it right away," she said as she showed herself out of his office. Her head raced with witty retorts but she pushed them back and reminded herself to swallow her pride. The most important thing in her world was keeping her brother safe. And it was for that reason that she needed to keep this job, no matter the frustrations—and temptations—of her new employer.

Two days later, though he'd tried to force her out of his head, Grant was still tormented by thoughts of his new personal assistant. He was supposed to be concentrating on a presentation by a potential new ad manager, but his mind kept wandering back to *her*. Jenna McCormick, he was quickly discovering, had the potential to be his undoing.

What was it about her that had him so distracted? Perhaps it was her flair for the unexpected. He'd expected to walk into the office on her first day and find her poised to seduce him. A low-cut blouse, a flip of the hair, a coy glance over her shoulder—that was the Jenna McCormick he'd expected to meet. Someone similar to the many women he'd dated—and usually regretted—countless times before. Instead, he'd gotten a buttoned-up, prim little secretary with pulled-back hair and next to no makeup, who within days had taught herself the phone and computer systems, deftly navigated the political waters of the office, and even managed to save him great expense on a derivative design. It threw him off his guard.

And he hated that. He'd built his career on staying focused and never misplacing his attention, and he wasn't about to let a spoiled heiress with a budgeting problem ruin that. *No matter how much sexual energy seemed to vibrate between them,* he added to himself grudgingly. Once again Grant found himself wishing he could be rid of her. Three months of Jenna's temptation could be too much, if he wasn't careful. But what choice did he have? He couldn't go back on his word now, not while she was doing a perfectly competent job as his assistant, and putting up with each and every request, no matter how inconveniencing, with aplomb. If he hoped to drive her out with his demands, he saw now that would be much harder than he'd imagined. If only there was another way he could prompt her to quit…

"Grant?" asked the ad manager, clearly noticing his lack of concentration. He looked up across the boardroom and really took in the woman talking to him for the first time. Dianne Framsworth had been strongly recommended to him by a board member. She was lithe, catlike, with a head full of tousled waves that he guessed took hours to put together, and a red mouth that spoke much more loudly than any words she could have used. In short, she was his type. So how had he failed to notice her existence until a half hour into the meeting? In fact, he hadn't heard a single word she'd said. He'd been too busy wondering what made Jenna McCormick tick—and why on earth he cared.

"I'm sorry, Dianne," Grant said, feeling defeated by his own mind, but refusing to let on the depth of his frustration. "I'm having trouble getting an office issue out of my head at the moment, and I think I've got to tend to it rather than give you anything less than my utmost attention." He'd return to his office and get the investigator on the phone—see what he'd dug up so far and confirm his impression of Jenna McCormick's motives. Then he'd be able to concentrate again. "Can I ask you to put forward some alternate times for the continuation of our meeting? I'll take you to my PA's desk to be scheduled right now." He rose, knowing he was being rude but not caring, unable to keep focus on anything but Jenna, and hating it.

"I understand completely," Dianne replied smoothly, leaning in closer to Grant, like a confidante. With one seductive motion, her shoulders rolled forward, letting her lacy camisole fall low on her cleavage. "You're passionate about your employees—it's an attractive quality in a man." As she spoke, she smiled coyly, as if she knew him well, even though they'd only just met.

So she was flirting with him. Typical. The woman who had come here to seduce him was sitting down the hall filing his paperwork, while the woman who was supposed to be conducting actual business was throwing herself at him shamelessly.

Ah, well. Who was he to deny an attractive—if somewhat aggressive—woman the pleasures of innocent flirtation? Perhaps she could help him forget his vexing personal assistant. He grinned like a wolf and gestured for Dianne to follow him down the hall with a light touch on her elbow, just slow enough to qualify as a caress. "And your flexibility is an attractive quality in a—" he paused, let her brain go where it might, and then finished, "—colleague. If you'll follow me?"

He escorted her down the long hallway toward the reception area, watched her play with her hair as they walked. He fussed over some imaginary speck of lint on his suit's lapel, but the normal charge he got from flirting with an attractive, interested woman was missing. He thought of taking Dianne out to some exclusive restaurant, lingering over a nice bottle of wine, and then going home together—but the idea held no interest for him. Then, unbidden, the thought of Jenna McCormick as his dinner date popped into his head, and he felt a tightness in his groin in response. *Dammit.* Jenna was the last woman in the world he should be thinking of.

As if conjured by his wayward thoughts, the very woman appeared at the end of the hallway, looking just as prim and proper as she had all day, and just as enticing. But when she spotted Dianne and Grant heading in her direction, the look on her face switched from her quiet confidence to shock. Openmouthed, she looked from Dianne to Grant, and then back to Dianne. Her eyes clouded over with some fierce emotion—could it be jealousy? And was that what he'd actually wanted?

JENNA SWALLOWED HARD when she saw the face of Grant's companion. *What was she doing here?* she wondered, then shook her head fiercely to bring herself back to the real world. Of course Dianne Framsworth would be darkening the hallways of McCormick Jewels—after all, hadn't her husband been on the very board that had dismissed Jenna once and for all? But Jenna could have sworn she'd heard through the grapevine that Dianne was now divorced. The way she was looking at Grant, as though he were the last man in the world, confirmed it—and, though she tried to ignore it, filled Jenna with irrational jealousy.

Before she could compose herself, Dianne's high singsong voice filled the hall. "Jenna McCormick!" she cried. "Why, what are you doing here?"

Dianne hardly let Jenna take a breath before she spoke again. "Well, of course, you're back at the company. How fantastic! When did they bring you back onto the board?"

Jenna flushed. Six years ago, before her parents died, Dianne had seemed like a best friend to her. But when she'd lost the company—and the high-flying lifestyle that went with it—Dianne had dropped her like a hot potato, moving on to other friends whose connections were better, whose outfits were newer and more fashionable. Now that she thought Jenna was back among the upper crust, of course she'd act like nothing had ever changed. It made Jenna cringe with embarrassment—for both of them.

"Actually, I'm not on the board," Jenna said, trying to keep her head held high.

"Upper management, then?" Dianne supplied. "I knew they'd forgive you for gambling like that with the company's stocks. It was naughty, and just plain dumb, of course, but it's not like you violated any actual laws or anything…" Her voice trailed off, as she at last noticed Jenna's narrowing stare.

"No, actually." Jenna straightened her shoulders and tamped down the flood of irritation. This was her chance to be a professional. To prove to Grant that she could handle this job. "I'm working here as the personal assistant to the CEO." She forced a smile as she gestured to Grant. "This is my third day on the job."

Dianne coughed politely. "Oh," she said, her voice no longer excited. "An assistant. I see." Jenna watched as Dianne looked at Grant helplessly, almost imploringly, as though he might somehow help her escape from this awkward situation. But Grant only stood there with a slightly amused look on his face.

In the silence, Jenna forced a smile, hoping it looked more genuine than it felt. "You're looking very well, Dianne," she said, saying the only nice thing she could think of in this situation. "You've hardly aged a day in six years."

"Oh, has it been that long?" Dianne asked, innocently. "My goodness. You know how it gets—our busy schedules. So much to do, so many fundraisers, and committees, and then fashion week, and…well, you know how it is. Or at least, you *used* to."

Hard as it was, Jenna forced herself to ignore the insult. She couldn't afford to let her temper get the best of her on her first week on the job. "Of course," Jenna said, as smoothly as she could, hoping her face wasn't turning too red.

"One of these days we should really get together and catch up."

That was the last thing in the world Jenna wanted to do, and for a moment she thought to tell Dianne so. But just then Grant seemed to come to her rescue, as though he sensed how close she was to breaking her composure.

"Jenna would never be so rude to say so, but she's got an absolutely packed schedule in these next weeks," he broke in smoothly. "The jewelers' convention, you know. I'm counting on her to work long hours in preparation."

"Yes," Jenna echoed gratefully, though the thought of working long hours in such close proximity to Grant made her uncomfortable in a completely different way. "Very long hours."

"I completely understand," Dianne said more to Grant than to Jenna, sounding just as relieved for the out as Jenna was.

"Now then, if we can get back to business. Dianne needs to reschedule—" Grant started, but with a wave of her arm the other woman cut him off.

"I think I'd better just have my assistant call in. She does my calendar anyway. Grant, see you soon?" Dianne touched his bicep seductively—a move that seemed to Jenna to be one last power play before she disappeared in a puff of smoke.

"Very well." To Jenna's surprise, he spoke curtly and pointed out the route to the elevator dismissively, bidding Dianne only the most businesslike of goodbyes. When she was gone, he turned to Jenna, eyebrows raised, a questioning look on his face. She thought of how he'd bailed her out just a moment ago and wanted to thank him, to explain why she and Dianne had such history, but he cut her off before she could get far. "I don't know what happened between the two of you in the past," he said brusquely, "and I don't care. Just be sure to keep holding onto that temper of yours, if you wish to keep this job." With that, he turned and stalked away.

ABOUT THE AUTHOR

Avery Laval writes romance novels and loves every minute of it. She lives in the midwest and teaches creative writing. She loves reading big stories and hanging out with small groups of friends.

She is the author of The Sin City Tycoons Series, which includes *A Tycoon's Jewel*, *A Tycoon's Rush*, and *A Tycoon's Secret*, all from Blue Crow Books. More Tycoons are coming in 2019!

Stay in touch with Avery through her author newsletter bit.ly/averylavalnews and her website www.averylaval.com.

facebook.com/averylaval

twitter.com/avery_laval

instagram.com/averylaval

goodreads.com/avery_laval

amazon.com/author/averylaval

bookbub.com/authors/avery-laval

CPSIA information can be obtained
at www.ICGtesting.com
Printed in the USA
BVHW04s0826040618
518140BV00001B/47/P